Bocas

Thomas M. Barron

Garbage Wagon LLC
San Francisco, CA

BOCAS

Cover art by David Powell
Creative Director Toby Petersen
Editor Maddy Hutchison

Published by
GARBAGE WAGON LLC
1720 Clay Street #8
San Francisco, CA 94109

This is a work of fiction. Names, characters, businesses, places, events and incidents are either the products of the author's imagination or used in a fictitious manner. Any resemblance to actual persons, living or dead, or actual events is purely coincidental.

Library of Congress Control Number: 2017918586
ISBN (print): 978-0-9997033-4-2
ISBN (ebook): 978-0-9997033-0-4

Printed in the United States of America
1 3 5 7 9 10 8 6 4 2

For _____ ,
Fuck (I miss) you.

1

Someone left a bump of coke on the top of the urinal. I finish, zip up and grab a towel. It seems like a waste to clean it up and throw it away, but there's already enough cocaine in Bocas.

Your job indicates that you are ruling at life when:

    a)   You have to commute by boat.

    b)   Drinking on the job is sanctioned.

    c)   Your boss is a cocaine trafficker.

    d)   All of the above.

My creepy boss, Raúl, is at the bar signing for a delivery. I start unloading the cases of Balboa cans and bottles down into the lateral fridge. Balboa is my favorite beer. It's also the most coveted beer here in Bocas del Toro, Panama.

"Jorge. Todo bien?" All good, George?

"Sí, claro."

"Qué no nadar aquí?" No swim today?

"No, no. Despues."

Normally, I have my Speedo drying on the railing. But I was running late and didn't have time. It's a mile across the bay to get here, and I can always swim on the way home. It's magic to swim at night. It's also a little thrilling to avoid the propellers of the homemade boat-taxis.

"Ah. OK. Luego."

Luego—see you later. This is the longest conversation I've ever had with Raúl, and his last word is superfluous. He could be back in five minutes, five hours or not at all.

But he doesn't need to worry about me stealing. If he even suspects that I'm skimming, my body will disappear off the face of the earth.

I know this, and he knows I know this.

Raúl in under twenty words: scary, shady, omnipresent, omni-absent, aloof, strong sense of justice, above average father and sometimes useful.

The thought of my bloody, third-world death flashes before my eyes.

I crack a beer.

I wonder if one of Raúl's associates supplied the coke that was on the urinal. Probably. Vertically integrated motherfucker.

I finish wiping down the bar and pop the lights on The Wreck.

El Barco Hundido isn't just a bar. It's an adult wonderland surrounding a sunken boat, hence—The Wreck Deck. It's a late night staple here in Bocas. A young gringo behind the bar gives the British backpackers a false sense of security, keeps them laughing and extracts U.S. Dollars from their wallets.

Raúl knows this, and he knows I know this.

A few minutes before 5pm, my roommate, PJ, pulls up in the S.S. Minnow—our shared Zodiac. It's got one of those lawnmower pull-type motors. Getting it started is such a hassle—it's no wonder I swim.

"You have a shirt on? And you're sober? What gives?"

"Barrel of monkeys arentcha, mate! Toss us a rope, ay?"

I tie up the skiff. He jumps onto the dock and picks me up in a bear hug. He's 5'8. I'm 6'3. Damn, he is strong.

PJ in under twenty words: unbelievably handsome, charming, simple, high-functioning alcoholic, a libido like Tommy Lee's drumstick and loyal as a Labrador.

PJ eyes my empty Balboa and lights up.

"Already on the piss? Good one! Pop us a couple Balbies, ay?"

A brief moment of hesitation. I drink for free. PJ does not. But PJ attracts a lot of paying customers—the women that will inevitably sleep with him and the guys that lurk, waiting like vultures for his vulnerable rebounds. He has a sense of entitlement, and it's not unwarranted. PJ thinks that he and Raúl are in a symbiotic relationship.

Raúl thinks that PJ is just a parasite.

I give in and crack two.

"Georgie, cheers!"

We each take a long pull and get mesmerized by the boat-taxi traffic.

It's rush hour.

"No licenses. No permits. No exhaust systems. Somehow, this never gets old."

He sucks down his beer. I follow, popping two more. These two, even colder than the last.

"Give us a proper cheers, in Español, ay?"

"OK. OK."

I tap the top of his beer, the bottom and the middle. "Nunca ariba, nunca abajo, siempre a tu lado." We each take a sip. He's giddy with anticipation, as I translate my eighth-grade Spanish. He knows this one, but he always waits for me to say it.

"Never above you. Never below you. Always beside you."

"Nice one!"

There is nothing more pleasurable than someone who is really easy to please.

•

At 1am, I lock up, drop my clothes, stick my tips in the safe, grab goggles and jump in the water. I'm already wearing a Speedo for underwear. The water feels amazing, and the sweaty bar filth disappears.

I drank eight beers over nine hours. Eight beers at work makes me sound like an alcoholic, but it's pretty normal. It's so hot here; you don't even glimpse a buzz, unless you drink a dozen Abuelo (rum) and Cokes.

After jumping in, I'm immediately thirsty, wishing I'd only drank seven. Even though it's late, the risk of a boat-taxi running me over is not zero. I stop and orient myself, by the lights from Bibi's Restaurant.

So thirsty.

I round the small bay of our compound and am greeted by two sounds: the guttural "WOOOGHF" of Wiglaf and the giggling of a skinny-dipping coed. It's textbook PJ. Thank god his room is on the other side of the house.

I reach the shallows and stand. Wiglaf watches me, stoically. Mind you, I feed this 130lb Rottweiler every single day.

The coed gasps, startled. Her twenty-two-year-old breasts bounce out of the water, and return, as PJ calms her.

"Welcome home, mate!" I wave and avert my eyes.

Still thirsty.

"Be careful, kiddies…"

"Ay…?" PJ only makes two types of statements. The ones ending in "mate" are the equivalent of double exclamation points. Similarly, the ones ending in "ay" (pronounced "aaaye") are double question marks.

PJ does not use periods.

It sounds annoying, but it's so simple. It's beautiful. For example, just now, the "Ay…?" didn't mean that he didn't understand me. It meant that he doesn't care—unless the police or bouncy coed's boyfriend are planning to show up.

I pound a quart of water.

Sleep.

•

I wake up, make coffee, pour some into the thermos for the boys, feed Wiglaf and check my email. How do I live on the sand, balls deep in the middle of Panama, and still have Wi-Fi?

Because of Israel.

Wiglaf's owner, Tsvika, is my other roommate and landlord. He's about as approachable as Raúl holding a lollipop.

Tsvika in under twenty words: mysterious—but in an uninteresting way—firm believer in quid pro quo, quiet, not a meddler and often useful.

Like many Israeli youths, Tsvika traveled for a year after his military service. After burning some time in Bocas del Toro, he coaxed his father into investing in property here, which he "manages." This story seems legit, but it's taken me the full eight months of living here to piece that together. Further, he's one of those guys that is always busy but never really doing anything concrete.

Did I mention that he's a bizarre, disappearing weirdo? And I wasn't kidding about the Raúl reference. I feel like Tsvika is made up of 51% good. Raúl? 49%. That 2% seems like nothing. But it's not.

Tsvika is how we live in a beachfront villa with satellite Wi-Fi.

The Wi-Fi is critical for my other job.

From: Rogers, Timothy

To: Georgeous

Subject: The next review cycle

George—

Thank you for your quick turnaround last week.

Unfortunately, Dan is on another college tour, so we won't get the next submission from his team until the last minute. I presume that won't be a problem, but I wanted to double check.

TR

PS How's the non-profit going? What is it again? Toys for Tots?

I make more coffee, pace and pet Wiglaf.

Tsvika named him after Beowulf's sentry—his trusty right-hand man. To me, Wiglaf is just a disturbing name that sounds like Big Death.

I walk off our porch and take a quick dip in the water.

Ahhh. Being submersed, even for ten seconds, drops my blood pressure. I towel off and head in to reply to TR.

Esquire Magazine contracted Dan Savage, from his syndicated *Savage Love* advice column. Once a week, Dan responds to two handpicked *Ask Esquire* emails. They get published on Esquire.com. Dan has a huge following, and they kill it in advertising revenue.

In school, TR and I used to work together at the *UCLA Daily Bruin*. Of course he was a talentless hack, and I was an underappreciated visionary. More accurately, TR's natural charisma helped him build a network like a Ponzi scheme, and that's what landed him his cushy job at Esquire.

Honestly? I'd kill a baby for his job. But he did toss me this easy proofreading gig. Sure, it was just to repay me for tightening up his *Bruin* articles, but I owe him one. TR is a true frenemy.

No lies, my spite is based on pure envy. But the proofing work only takes twenty minutes a week. Savage's work is solid, and his team's writing is really crisp. Plus, they pay me a bonus to kick off each piece with a quiz or brief love advice vignette.

I secretly love this bit.

Sometimes, I'll spend hours pointlessly over-editing it. TR knows he can't find anyone he trusts for cheaper. And I know I can't make $400/month in a few hours' work, with my feet in the sand, anywhere else.

From: Georgeous

To: Rogers, Timothy

Subject: At your service

TR—

Numerically:

1. My pleasure.
2. No problem.
3. Similar acronym, similar target audience—different outcome. It's Teach Them To Swim—the same non-profit you donated $200 to at Christmastime. Belated thank you.

Best,

George

Pretty good, right? That only took five rewrites.

His $200 donation was gigantic. It brought TTTS.org to a whopping $843 total—making TR the one true TTTS benefactor. I'm appreciative, but it still stings.

PJ rolls into the kitchen. He's holding his budget island cellphone, which means he's already texted Emanuel to come pick up the coed in a boat-taxi.

PJ is a creature of habit.

"G'day, mate!"

"Mornin'." PJ goes straight for the coffee. Coed saunters in, fresh from the shower, wearing a slightly-too-tight tank top.

Shocker.

"Hi! I'm Jasmine!"

"Hey there. George. Sorry to startle you guys last night."

"Oh, no problem! You did scare me, though!"

"Ah, babe! I would have saved you!" PJ goes in for the awkward post-hookup kiss. But she digs it.

"So, PJ says you SWIM here from the bar? No way! Isn't that dangerous? It's sooo far!"

"Nah, it's not too bad. Especially at night, when the taxi traffic dies down. Do you want some coffee?"

"Sure. Thanks!"

PJ looks out toward the dock, keeping an eye out for Emanuel, hoping she doesn't linger too long.

We chat for a bit. The sound of an outboard motor creeps up, pulling us out to the dock. PJ and Jasmine hug-kiss misfire. I'm unsure why I decided to walk out with them. Emanuel is rock solid and helps her into the boat, without the slightest coy smile or snicker.

"Byeee! Facebook me, okaaay?!"

"Sure thing, love!"

We watch them pull away.

"You should be registered with the Center for Disease Control."

"Ay?"

"Never mind."

"Fancy a dip mate? Maybe after some brekkie? I'm famished!"

Of course he's starving after last night. And, of course, he can't cook.

I fire up the eggs and my custom casamiento recipe—rice and beans cooked with whatever vegetables that we have left in the fridge. Tsvika emerges from his cave downstairs and grabs a mug.

"Tsviks? Want some breakfast? We're down to two eggs apiece, but there's plenty of rice and beans."

"Thanks. No."

And our little dance begins.

I ask. He declines. I leave him a plate. He devours it. We return later to find clean dishes and a spotless kitchen.

Weirdo.

•

PJ and I walk around the bay to El Morro Negro. PJ has his board, and I've got my fins. His long curly locks and shirtless physique make him look like a beardless, shorter version of Poseidon.

It took months, but my feet have finally adjusted to the reef scrapes, red ant bites and flip-flop rash. I can't believe the Lonely Planet doesn't have an entire chapter on foot hazards. It's brutal.

Even with the built-up callouses, I constantly scan the path for that one tarantula that's got my number. And damn if those hidden tree crabs don't look similar.

The crabs bite, too.

We've been in the water for all of twelve seconds, and PJ drops into a ten-foot bomb—shredding like it's his job. Sometimes we take the boat over to Bastimientos, to surf the beach breaks. If it's not too big, I'll take a longboard out and try to surf with PJ. But sitting on a board, next to a pack of intense locals, and jockeying for waves that break over a reef is way out of my league. That's why I bodysurf with fins.

Safer.

PJ paddles up next to me, grinning ear-to-ear.

"Let's go, mate! Kiddies in school! The point is ours!" He's right. Half of the normal crowd is in school. I didn't even notice, because it's hard to remember what day it is here.

I trail behind him, kicking a little lackluster, fearful of the big outside sets.

And here they come.

I duck under a few monsters, appreciative of the burst of power I get from the fins. An eighteen-year-old kid drops in right in front of me, looking like he's going to slice my face off with his board.

Reaching PJ, his eyes are fixed on the horizon.

"It's getting bloody corduroy! Look at them come!"

Uh oh.

A picture perfect wave lines up, right in front of us. PJ turns to take it but stops. He barks at me.

"GO GO GO!" I take two strokes, kick hard and fully commit. I reach a hand out to glide along the face. Perfect.

I hear PJ scream behind me.

"WOOOHOOO!"

Some people think bodysurfing is easy. It's not.

It keeps going and going. I can see the reef beneath me. Normally, I would have pulled out by now. But instead, I kick to stay in it, driving down the line. It's scary. And completely magical.

The lip peels over my head. My right hand digs behind me, like a rudder. Full-blown barrel. The taste of my heart beating in my mouth pauses, for three perfect seconds.

Thump.

The wave closes out. My scrawny body drags across the reef. I try to lie flat, so I don't get cut too badly. Instantly, the saltwater tells me that I have three cuts. I couldn't care less. I swim into the channel and rejoin PJ.

"Nice one! Epic!"

I smile like a giddy child, pleased at his approval.

He turns and paddles toward the far peak. I pick off a few easy ones, close to shore.

Walking home, blood trickles from my knee and elbow.

"You got nicked up, ay?"

"Yeah, a bit. But I'd do it again in a second. Amazing."

"That's a good mate! You've got the bug!" His eyes sparkle with untamed glee. His fearlessness defines him.

We round the corner toward our little bay, and PJ looks back at the point.

"You'll nevah forget yah first one. Nevah!" And I know he's right.

I can't stop smiling.

Ouch! Fucking red ants.

•

"WOOOGHF." Hi, Wiglaf.

Dabbing at a cut on my elbow with my finger, I'm hoping Shawna's triple antibiotic cream hasn't expired.

I shower and rifle through a bag I haven't opened in months. There it is—the first aid kit Shawna gave me as a going away present.

Shawna.

I slap on antiseptic. Thinking of her makes me crave her. She looks like she could be from anywhere—Cairo, Morocco, New York City. But, like me, she's from nowhere, and that's even more tantalizing.

Erection.

I yank the towel off and go at it.

Shawna.

Picturing her long wild hair dragging across her chest…that's all it takes. Ninety seconds in and I unleash on my stomach—in four pent-up bursts.

I look down.

Whoa.

My man-juice is an exact replica of the famous Air Jordan silhouette. I lay back, motionless, taking it in. It's tempting to photograph it, but what would I do with the photo?

Number 23 himself would not be amused.

If Shawna and I were still together, she'd think it was hilarious and be incredibly flattered; she's a huge basketball fan.

Reluctantly, I clean it off. The morning heat takes me. My eyelids feel heavy, wanting a nap.

As I doze, I wonder if my old Air Jordan high-tops are still in a box in my mom's house in Pasadena. I need to send her a postcard.

I've stopped emailing with my mom, because she's picked up that horrific abbreviated text-speak from her students. For example:

R U Safe? Miss U. Hope to C U soon.
Mom

No one over twenty-eight should write like this, especially my mother. She teaches Advanced Grammar at Pasadena City College. It's shameful. I just turned twenty-nine, and I try to hold myself to a higher standard. At least grammatically.

Sleepily walking into the kitchen, I see PJ, already drinking his first beer at 11:30am. What can I say? It's fucking Bocas.

He pushes a large FedEx box a few inches toward me, across the kitchen island.

"Happy Christmas, mate!" I can't keep myself from reading his t-shirt.

"I know it wouldn't fit, but please now, or in thirty years, please put that t-shirt in your will for me. I love it. Absolutely love it."

PJ, a man completely devoid of irony, wears the most clever novelty t-shirts.

This one: *Fuck You. Balloons are Cool.*

PJ's family owns a silk-screening business in Australia. I can't tell whether he picks each t-shirt for its clever pun or if he just wears whatever didn't sell.

"Awww, mate! What happened to being anti-sentimental, ay?"

"That was anti-nostalgic. Regardless, if I have to fly to your funeral Down Under to get that shirt, I will. Even if it takes pulling it off your brother's back."

"Ahhh, don't get so hectic! It's yours!"

He yanks it over his shoulders and sets it on the counter, knowing I won't take it. Showing off his muscles right on cue—he does this all day long.

"Look! Santa came early!"

He brandishes a kitchen knife. I nod, letting him open it.

Tilting the box, out pours a river of goggles—adult's, children's, clear, anti-reflective—top of the line.

I wrote to Speedo to see if they'd sponsor TTTS. They conducted a perfunctory check of my 501c3 non-profit status (it's so easy to set up; it's a joke) and have now dropped the mother lode—at least a hundred sets of goggles, flotation devices, kickboards and a ton of other swag that I didn't even ask for.

God, I hope one of these Speedos will fit. All of mine are two hand-washes away from disintegrating.

I'm so grateful. Speedo granted me $1,500 worth of gear, renewable for up to three years. Killer, right? One catch—they wouldn't pay for shipping. Some weird tax clause or something. Shipping this box to Bocas would cost $450.

I was whining about it to PJ a few weeks back, with Tsvika

eavesdropping.

"Your grant? The swimming company?"

"Yeah, I got it."

"Good." Said with zero enthusiasm.

"It's awesome, but I have to pay for shipping. So it's not happening."

"How much? It cost? The shipping?" Sometimes I wonder if his abrupt speech is due to English being his second language or if he's always this terse, even in Hebrew. Probably both.

"All in? With taxes? Nearly $500. I need to write them back and decline or find some other way."

"What you need? The FedEx?"

"Yeah, or a DHL number. Why? Do you have a connection?"

"Probably no. But I check. Wait two days, eh?"

"OK. Thanks so much, man."

You know how when most people say yes, they mean maybe, and when they say maybe, they mean no? Well, Tsvika always starts with no, which still sometimes means yes. Then, "I look at it. No promising." This unilaterally means yes. His access to resources—aka satellite Wi-Fi on an isolated Caribbean island—makes the fact that he's a complete weirdo much more palatable.

PJ cracks open a pair of pink children's goggles.

"The Tsviks got you sorted, ay?"

"Yeah, his connections are sick. Check it out!" I rifle through the bounty.

Ten days ago, Tsvika left a note on the fridge. No pleasantries, just:

G—

Use this one.

T

With a FedEx number.

Awesomeness.

PJ puts the goggles on upside down and starts walking around the house like a transvestite Frankenstein. The pink suits him.

•

Bocas del Toro is a group of islands in Panama, bordering Costa Rica, on the Caribbean side. It started out as a banana plantation. It eventually became popular with Costa Rican expatriates, both as a quaint getaway and also as a convenient spot to renew a passport.

The "green gold" of bananas transitioned into tourism. Thanks to the empty white sand beaches, $1 beers and incredible nightlife, the conversation has gone from "What should I do? I'm here for a week?" to "Are you guys hiring?" Even U.S. retirees have gotten the memo. Land and healthcare are much cheaper here than in Florida.

Me? I'm mostly in Bocas because of Shawna.

•

Shawna.

Shawna in under two words: complex.

She sat in the bleachers and read books, while I gave lessons at the YMCA pool in South Pasadena. She nannied for two rich rug rats. I'd seen her about fifteen times before we finally met.

"Hi!"

"Hey there. Staying dry?"

"Trying!"

"How's the Bingham?"

"What?"

"Your book. *Lightning on the Sun*. You like it?"

"You know it? It's amazing. Dark, though."

"Yeah, I thought so, too. But I loved it."

"It's impossible that you could read the cover from the kiddie pool. What is that? Fifty feet?"

"I've walked by you a dozen times now. And it's impossible that you did not notice me flexing."

"HA! Ummm…I didn't. But that's super weird and kinda sweet."

All I could think about was holding her hand. And seeing her naked.

"You're Damien and Devin's mom, right?" Holy yuppie names. I knew she wasn't—too young and no ring—but I was baiting her.

"What? I am not their MOTHER! I'm just the nanny!" Her eyes popped open. I wanted to dive into them.

"I know. I'm teasing."

She snickered, playfully, and threw me a bone.

"They adore you, you know."

"And I hate them."

"No you don't!"

"No, I don't. They're great boys. But I kinda do, just a little."

"Yeah, me too."

Time for class.

•

One night, I lay awake trying to figure out how to get the kids away from us.

At 4am, I rolled out of bed. I hit the lights and scoured the bookshelf. Finally, I picked *A Prayer for Owen Meany*. On the first page I wrote:

I'd like to spend some time with you.
George

I wanted to say so much more. That she was funny. That she was beautiful. That I was impressed by how well she connected with children—something I personally struggle with—even though I teach fucking swim lessons. But my feelings were really that simple. I closed the book and slept like a baby.

Lessons were only twice a week.

I had to wait.

2

How to court a woman:

> *Pretty women want to hear that they're smart. Smart women want to hear that they're pretty. The trick? Expressing both.*

"Damien! Great job today, buddy!"

"I went all the way across, BY MYSELF!"

"I know you did!"

"Did you see me?"

"I did! Hey, can you do me a little favor?"

"When am I gonna be a Goldfish?"

"Well, you just became a Guppy. Remember a week ago, when you were a Tadpole?"

"Devin's already a Goldfish!"

"I know he is. And Devin's a year older than you. He's been

swimming longer. Right?"

"I wanna be a Goldfish…"

"You will be soon, little buddy. Real soon, I promise. Now, do me a favor, OK?" I held the book toward the wall, away from the splashing little hellions.

"I WANNA BE A GOLDFISH!"

"You're gonna be a Goldfish so soon! You just need to learn how to hold your breath under water for five seconds. Do you wanna practice with me next week?"

"GOOOLDFISH!!!!!"

It was already too late.

Complete implosion. Tears. Wailing. He dropped onto the concrete (ouch) and thrashed about.

There was nothing I could do.

Parents, grandparents and nannies were arriving—full of enthusiasm for the Intermediate Barracudas (cool name, huh?) class. They'd singsong words of encouragement, "Are you going swimming today?! Oh yes you are!" Their revelry was usurped by Damien's ear-piercing meltdown.

Shawna stepped in.

"Damien Anheuser Branham! Stop that! Right now!" Yes, the little bastard was a distant heir to the Budweiser Anheuser-Busch empire. The King of Beers brings you the Prince of Brats.

"Damien!" His wails subsided. She picked his little broke ass up.

"Now, you apologize to Coach Lewis!" He balked. "Apologize. NOW."

Even I was scared.

"Mmm sooorrry…" He muffled through her snot-drenched scarf. Where did she buy that scarf? Mauritius? Katmandu? It turned out to be Target.

She wasn't budging. I should have paid more attention at this moment—a foreshadowing of our future fights.

"Again. And look him in the eye."

The black stretch pants and diamond wearing yuppie moms stuck around, either for the drama or the parenting tips. Probably both. Damien peeked one eye out.

"I'm sooorrry, Coach Lewis."

I reflexively reached and stroked his back.

"No problem, little buddy. I'll see you on Thursday. Now practice in the bathtub, like I showed you. OK?"

"Okaaay."

Shawna half-turned and spoke softly.

"I'm so sorry. He didn't get his nap today."

"No problem at all. Par for the course…" But she was already carrying him away.

•

There were only four classes left that summer. I couldn't let Damien box me out again. This time I came in hot, at the start of class.

"Hey there!"

"Hey!"

I held out the book.

"You should check this out sometime."

"Irving. One of my favorites." She flipped through the pages like a deck of cards and handed it back to me. "It's great, but I've already read it. Thank you for thinking of me."

Damn.

"Coach Lewis! Can we use the floaties today? PLEEEASE?" Little Aiden (yes, another yuppie name) was killing my mojo. I half-turned toward him.

"Aiden, we're doing leg kicks today. Grab a kickboard, OK?" I turned back toward smug Shawna. Who really waits for a response from a child, anyway?

"I think you should at least…" She cut me off.

"Do you always start your book clubs in a Speedo?" She looked directly at my package.

Ooof.

My game was gone. I took one last shot.

"At least just…just reread the first page. OK?"

"Sure thing, Coach Lewis."

Who is this chick?

Flustered, I walked down the pool deck, toward my kids. Left alone for two minutes, they were already creating mayhem. Turning right at the lane lines, I couldn't help but glance back. She'd opened the book and turned to the first page. Her eyes widened, and she mouthed, "Ohhh…"

She looked up at me, closed the book and smiled.

Victory.

"Hi, guys! Who can show me that they remember how to blow

bubbles?"

"I CAN!"

•

The Wreck Deck has been open for an hour, and there's not a soul in sight. It's Cartoon Hamburger's last night in town. I won't bother translating their names into Spanish—they're all gringos. Who else could afford electric guitars and amps? They're playing a farewell set at La Iguana. The whole island will be there.

Raúl's son, Marco, sits idly, slowly ripping napkins into pieces. He's destructive, in an obedient sort of way. He knows not to incur his father's wrath. We can hear the Heepheepheep sound of the ice cream man riding by, honking the horn on his BMX bike.

Marco doesn't even bother asking his dad for a treat.

Señor Helado's little clown horn is the most annoying sound in the world. Raúl's scowl tells me that he agrees.

I call him Marquito, because when his dad isn't around, he follows me around like a mosquito. Thank god it sounds exactly like Marcito, the Spanish slang for Little Marco, otherwise Raúl might slit my throat at the offense. The nicknames are endless here, including mine: Flacito (for my skinny, lanky build), Jorge and Jortuga (sounds like Hortuuuga). Idiot savant that he is, PJ nicknamed Raúl "The Praúler," since he's always showing up unannounced, recounting his money and disappearing.

Genius.

I have a new set of goggles for Marquito, and they're burning a hole in my pocket. He's going to go apeshit. But I have to wait for the right time. Raúl passively appreciates my watchful eye over Marco, but he doesn't want me spoiling him.

Marquito is eight. His mom died two years ago from cervical cancer. It's not unlikely that she contracted HPV from Raúl, given the number of prostitutes he sleeps with.

"Ya terminaste? Con el inventario?" Inventory all done?

"Sí, ayer." Inventory was yesterday, and he knows it.

"Quieres ir? Es tranquilo." It's slow tonight. You can take off, if you want.

I would love the night off.

"Sí, por favor." I haven't had a Saturday night off in forever, and it'd be fun to blow off some steam. I know PJ is probably already four beers deep, ripping his shirt off.

I ask if I can take Marco for a quick swim, whispering, so Marco doesn't hear. Even though it's 8pm, it's still crazy hot. I can't wait to get in the water. It'll also make Marquito's day.

Raúl dismisses me with his hand. If you want, gringo. He goes back to his logbook.

I walk over to Marquito, with my hands behind my back.

"Recoges una mano." Pick a hand.

He hesitates. Then he taps my right arm. I switch the goggles into my right hand, still behind my back, and hand them to him.

"Mía?" Mine?

"Sí, regalito." Yep. A little present.

He looks over at his father, to see if he'll take them away. Raúl gives an approving nod.

"Gracias!" He holds them delicately. So cute.

Swimming is the only thing that makes little Marco smile. Maybe that's why I'm so soft for him.

Raúl whistles, firmly eyeing the paper napkin boneyard on the bar. Marquito obediently picks up every single scrap, throws them away and is right back at my heels. Maybe one day Raúl could drop in and teach a parenting class at the Y.

We dive in at the dock. I know that some of the toilets flush directly into this water, but you wouldn't guess as much, given how crystal clear it is. I tread water and fix Marco's goggles. I suck in a deep breath, and Marco mimics. We dive down and survey the fish, discarded boat motor pieces and abundant orange starfish. It looks like The Little Mermaid meets Sanford and Son.

We come back up, and Marco is gasping. Goddamn, the water feels good. Marco catches his breath. I wait for it, and he's right on cue.

"Jortuga?"

"Ahhh…" I've gotta reel him in a little. He knows I'll give in.

"Por favooor?"

"OK."

"JORTUGA!" He climbs on my back. I exhale all of the air from my lungs. He sucks down all he can hold, and then we drop.

To get the YMCA kids to advance to the next level, I'd take the intermediate students on "ride the turtle" cruises. It's not complicated. They'd jump on my back, and we'd swim down into the deep end. But I'd only do it at the end of class and only if they were good, which was not often. In the classes I've held in Panama, turtle became Tortuga, combined with my local name—Jorge—Jortuga.

I equalize my eardrums, by pinching my nostrils and adding pressure. Marco imitates.

We do Jortuga a few times. I have another local class coming up, and no one gets the premium treatment like Marco. But when your father is a drug trafficker and your mom is dead, you should get a few freebies.

I'm spent.

"Más, más!" More, more!

"No Marquito, terminado." He gives a tiny pout, but he knows not to argue when grown-ups say no. If he'd grown up in the States, in a decent neighborhood, he could have become an investment banker. His adaptability and observation skills far surpass his age.

But he's here.

So he's fucked.

I pop up onto the dock and catch Raúl receiving a grip of cash from the scariest mofo I've ever seen. I pretend not to notice and yank Marquito up. He takes off his goggles and holds them tightly in both hands. He keeps looking down, checking to make sure they're still there.

It breaks my heart.

It's just past dusk, and Raúl hits the lights on The Wreck. I've worked here for months, and it remains the coolest thing I've ever seen. Cold drinks atop a sunken ship—it's magical. Marquito also looks longingly. I can hear him telepathically. In my mind, we only speak in English.

"I want to do George-tuga down there! Whoa!"

"Me too, little man, me too."

•

The Iguana is raging. Miracle—PJ has his shirt on. No miracle—he's surrounded by three attractive tourists from Spain. All three are licking their chops at him. He's got his eyes on the one that looks like Salma Hayek. PJ must have used up his eight words of Español. And he is wasted.

"Georgie!" Big bear-hug pick up, off the floor, etc. They giggle. This whole scene sounds cliché, but it's bananas how well he pulls it off.

"Buenas tardes. Me llamo Jorge. Mucho gusto."

"Aye! Tú hablas Español?!" They're shocked that I know a little Spanish, but surpassing PJ is not difficult.

"Sí, un poco."

"Pero su amigo? Naaada." I used to hound PJ about learning at least a little Spanish, out of respect. But why would he bother? He has no incentive. He never sleeps alone.

"Sí, mi compañero…"

This is the process of PJ hooking up—he starts telling stories, which I translate, while he simultaneously pantomimes. The three of them talk directly back to him, which I translate, and he makes editorial comments, which I also attempt to translate.

Their names are Alejandra, Vanesa and Camila. Since the V in Vanesa is pronounced as a B, their initials are close enough to A, B and C. I am terrible with names and will use any trick I can.

PJ's banter sounds absurd, but he mostly tells stories about me, which involve a lot of him showing off his smile and muscles. Very effective.

And here he goes.

"Girls, girls, girls! My mate Georgie here can hold his breath for two minutes! TWO BLOODY minutes! Show them, Georgie!"

"Qué?"

Most of my translation sounds like, "Roommate PJ, mine? Yes of his words discussing breath of me longish minutes two sometimes practicing always, yes?"

They handle it graciously.

"Verdad?!" Seriously?!

"Mate! You've gotta show them! Show them! Give us yah wristwatch, ay?" There's no point in fighting it. Plus, it's a pretty dope party trick.

I hand him my watch.

Everyone within ten feet of us is following this unorthodox mating ritual. A small crowd surrounds us for the countdown. Short-ass PJ steps up onto a barstool.

"READY?"

"Can I have a shot first?" I don't even want one, but let's build it up a little.

"'COURSE, MATE!"

Fifteen shots are poured for the small crowd.

"Up yah bum!"

We put them down. The bartender served us the cheesy tourist shot—El Loco del Toro—all sugar, no alcohol. I pour these bad boys all night at The Wreck. I want to judge, but I'm happy it's not Jameson.

"Yah ready mate?"

"Yep."

I skip his intro and inhale.

"GO!"

He hits the stopwatch. Spanish A, V and C follow, each taking a deep breath.

Pretty damn cute.

I close my eyes and go to my happy place. First, I try to sink to the bottom of the bay in front of our house and lie in the sand. It doesn't work. A little burp of air slips out.

Whoops.

"THIRTY!"

I need to focus, or I won't make it. Alejandra and Vanesa tap out. I try hard not to, but my mind is weak. And my heart is weaker. Especially when it comes to finding calm, comfort.

Shawna.

I'm spooning her. Dozing. My chin rests on her shoulder. Her hair is pulled up, away, over the pillow.

Camila taps out around fifty-five seconds. Pretty impressive.

"SIXTY!"

I feel my heart rate slow. A strand of Shawna's hair drags across my nose. Even though I'm in fantasy land, I scratch it. Vanesa gasps, thinking I'm done.

"NINETY SECONDS!"

Some surfer backpacker pipes up.

"Holy shit, bro! That guy is crushing it!"

I reach my hand and rest it on Shawna's hip. She sighs. I can feel myself falling asleep. I teeter against the barstool.

"TWO MINUTES!" I grit my teeth, as I start to wake from the spell. My chest clenches. I reach for Shawna's thigh.

Camila rests her hand on my arm.

"La puta madre!" Motherfucker is right. My stomach starts to revolt. My lungs heave.

"TWO THIRTY!" My eyes pop. That's all I've got. I open my mouth and suck in deeply, like Willie Nelson's first bong hit.

"Two and a half mate! Bloody incredible!"

Camila moves closer and rubs my chest.

"Todo bien? Muy impresionante!" Her sweet touch erases Shawna. I'm thankful.

She offers me a drink, and I wish I could speak Spanish well enough to quickly spit out: "Yes, but please, whatever you do, don't take your hands off of me."

She does, but they come back.

Half an hour later, PJ is devouring the lips off of Alejandra. He gives her the let's go nod.

She's ready.

Normally, part of his pitch is, "Come check out our beachside villa, ay?" Which is pretty enticing when the other option is going back to her hostel and sleeping on a bunk bed.

But Alejandra doesn't need the full sales pitch—she's in.

"Don't forget that you have to draw the flyer tomorrow. They've gotta get posted by Sunday, or no one will come."

PJ used to do graphic design for the family business, before we met in Panama and both decided to stay on permanent vacation. I'm hoping he doesn't stay up all night, so that he can finish the TTTS handout for the workshop by tomorrow morning. It can take two days to get them printed in town.

It's a bummer that he'll never see her again after tonight, because they look oddly happy together. Their children would be beautiful.

"Ahhh, 'course, mate! I'm right as rain!"

"OK. OK. Thanks, dude. Sorry to pester."

"No worries! Hey, you'd better pick one quick! They're either going to kill each other or start rooting right here in the bar!"

He's right. Vanesa and Camila have gotten into the most intense discussion. They are cousins and have an incredible chemistry. Both are rub/scratch/petting me like a dog as they chat. I tried getting a few words in, but it feels so good to be touched—I don't even care.

The bartendress at The Iguana knows me from The Wreck and keeps dropping off free beers, laughing at my predicament. Vanesa reaches under my shirt and lightly drags her nails down my back. She tells Camila that her little sister borrowed her skirt and didn't give it back. That was her favorite skirt! You know, the one that made her legs look nice!

There's a rumor that Castilian, one of the dialects spoken in Spain, has such a strong "th" sound because, a few centuries ago, the King of Spain had a lisp. When Vanesa says plaza, it sounds like "platha," with the "th" in the middle lasting for about a month. They've moved on to the Kardashians (who knew they were so globally relevant?). Normally, I'd wanna kill myself, but she keeps saying Los Kardathians, and it's fantastic.

Her nails are now at the waistband of my shorts. We need to get out of here. Camila starts talking about Khloé's ass, and without missing a beat, reaches for the bar, hands me a fresh beer, and starts going on about Kim ("Keeem"), while tapping my sternum for emphasis.

A perfect moment.

This beer is a Soberana. The name is not ironic—Soberana means sovereign in Spanish, not sober. This means they've run out of Balboa. It's time to go. All of the beers here are like khakis from Gap or Banana Republic—the exact same pants, just a different label. But somehow, the Banana Republic ones feel sharper, right? That's how I feel about Balboa.

"Tengo que ir. Quiere que se acompañe a su hotel?" I've gotta go. Want me to walk you home?

"Sí! Muy caballeroso!" It's like they've been waiting for me to ask them for an hour. My lack of intuition is staggering.

Are we about to have a sleepover? I hope so.

God, I should have skipped those last few beers. Walking arm-in-arm down Avenue C, we avoid the trash and rusty pieces of metal that make you crave a tetanus shot. My foot kicks an empty bottle of bleach, and they overdramatize their concern.

"Con cuidado, guapo!" Careful, handsome!

Trash, attractive tourists, flip-flop hazards—a typical day here in Bocas.

And that's why everyone loves it here.

We've arrived. I can't decide if this place is an upscale hostel or a shitty hotel.

Same thing.

We skip the *Do you want me to come in?* bit, and they drag me inside—such a timesaver. Vanesa mixes Coke, vodka and three ice cubes apiece. Gross. Camila runs her fingers through my hair like I'm McDreamy, which I'm not. I take a courtesy sip of my drink. It's awful, but it's cold. Maybe vodka and Coke should be the Ladies' Night drink at The Wreck.

Vanesa casually lays a leg over my lap and starts peppering words at Camila, "Did you ask, him? I'm sure it's fine. Just ask him!"

Camila hesitates. She looks me in the eye—dead serious. "Bueno. Estamos practicando, eh…cómo se dice…el bloh yab? Me entiendes?"

"You guys are practicing your blow job?"

"Sí! Bloh yab! Quieres?" *Do you want one?* She's not being rhetorical.

I won't bother translating my answer. They both start undoing my pants, with purpose. My body feels like a middle school science project. It doesn't really feel sexual, so I ask them to take their shirts off. Camila responds, all business, by mechanically taking her shirt off and expediting the same for Vanesa.

Vanesa starts stroking me. Simultaneously, she teases Camila about how a mole on her boob looks like the Spanish island of Majorca. It does.

I try to kiss them. Three times. But they'd rather talk to each other and use my penis as a workbench. I sit back and look back and forth between their boobs.

Vanesa takes me in her mouth; Camila coaches from the sidelines. "No, no, get the side, first. Cup the huevos." I have to paraphrase here, as they're using a lot of slang terms that I don't know.

After a few minutes, Camila gets fed up and takes over.

"Mira, mira, mira…" Look look, look… Aka—watch me do it.

Whoa. She is committed. I swear she has the entire thing in her mouth, but I can't tell for sure. I'm so curious. I want to tell her that she doesn't have to do that. It must be so uncomfortable.

Vanesa studies and nods approvingly. She keeps her drink with her and mentally calculates: boobs + boys = orgasm.

Correct.

She sits up on her heels and offers a nipple to my lips. I take it. This would be perfect, but all I can hear is the sound of her swallowing the vodka and Coke. Did she just glance over my head at the TV?

Camila stops for a second and uses her sexy voice.

"Córrete…" Come for me. Of course she wants me to come. She must be exhausted.

"Ahh. OK. OK. Un poco más despacio, por favor?" I feel rude asking her to slow down, but we're all about timesaving tonight. She goes at half speed. Perfect.

Here it comes.

I tap Camila's shoulder frantically, giving her the option to eject.

She doesn't.

Ahhh.

And the first threesome of my life reaches completion. Nine minutes, all in. I lean back against the couch, savoring the moment.

About fifteen seconds of silence passes, before they start breaking it down.

"Did you see how I used my hand to push and pull, as I go down on the tip?"

"Yeah, I did. You're a real professional."

Vanesa tightens our drinks up, and Camila puts her bra back on, heading toward the bathroom. I close my eyes and take a mini nap.

Vanesa sets a drink down on the glass. It wakes me. The sparring starts back up.

"You know your brother has never had a real job."

"He's an artist!"

"He's a loser."

I can't figure out whether I should stay or to go. I almost feel used. My heart aches for every mistreated woman on earth. But Vanesa snaps me out of it. She strips down to her panties and puts her sleeping shirt on.

Her brother does sound like a loser.

"Guapo, estás dormido?" Camila invites me to bed, and the three of us triple spoon. It's bliss for two minutes. Until they start talking. Again.

Jesus.

But Vanesa is back to tickling my back with her nails. I settle in.

I wake up four hours later, tasting my bad dehydrated breath and needing to pee. I slink out of bed.

Vanesa whispers.

"Adiós, Jorgito. Cierra la puerta en su salida, OK?" She remembered my name. I'm impressed. But, lock the door on your way out? It's 6:55am.

I pause, confused.

Cuddling up, they erase my spot in the bed. They whisper to each other and giggle. In my mind, I hear Vanesa say, "Ahhh, he wants to snuggle! Pobrecito..." Then their giggling turns to laughter.

They're laughing at me. And I'm not imagining it.

They've made it clear that getting back into bed is not an option.

Poor baby is right. I close the door behind me, feeling like a whore.

I won't be able to get a boat back to our house on Carenero for at least another hour. That's if I'm lucky—it's Sunday.

The morning sun is bright, but it's quiet out. It lets me coddle my bruised ego, with Bocas still asleep. A vacant lot acts as a welcome bathroom. I post up next to a huge decaying truck and unzip.

I hurry, recognizing my sanctuary as a welcoming haven for big spiders.

I walk downtown. One of the locals-only places is open. The entire restaurant is three street-side barstools.

"Buenas. Un cafecito, por favor?" It's nice to have someone else make coffee.

"Sí, sí. Quires desayuno, tambien?" Coffee? Of course. Breakfast?

"Oh, sí. Huevos con chorizo, por favor." I'm hoping that the sausage and eggs will cure my hangover.

She pours a glass of filtered water for me and tells me to drink it, to offset the heat.

It's unusually hot for 7am, and I'm thankful for the water. In Bocas water is precious. And expensive. This glass of filtered water cost her more than the eggs. It's this kind of recurring kindness—seeking zero reciprocation—that keeps me here.

I respect, admire and love the people of Panama.

But then, last night's bizarre conclusion creeps in. The malaise makes me slouch on the stool while I eat.

Alone.

3

A female sleeps over and gets naked. In the morning you:

　　a)　Fake an 8am commitment, leave the house and lurk around the corner.

　　b)　Tell her you're still too drunk to drive and order her an Uber.

　　c)　Same as b, but you step it up to a premium vehicle.

　　d)　Ask her if she wants to hang out tomorrow night.

While moving the swim lane lines before class, Damien runs into me.

"Hey, buddy. Slow down on the pool deck. OK?"

"COACH LEWIS! Shawna told me to give this to you!" He hands me the book back.

I'm a little bummed that she had him do it. But I look down and see something sticking out of the top. Damien races off. I don't have the energy to tell him to slow down.

I open it.

It's a hand-drawn bookmark. She must've had it laminated at Staples. It's a rough sketch of the pool, viewed from the bleachers. She used the back of the Summer Aqua Aerobics Schedule. I'm impressed, because she must have drawn it here. And not just here, based on the date, she had to have drawn it the last time we spoke.

Her sweetness hits my heart like a velvet sledgehammer.

I remove the bookmark and see a note written underneath mine:

Me too.
Shawna

With her number.

•

Other than a handful of days, we spent every night together for six months.

Fucking, fondling, fighting. I would hate her for ten minutes. Then I would smell her deodorant on the shoulder of my shirt—leftover from our drawn-out morning goodbye ritual. Instantly, I'd start craving her. I'd wait for her to get off work, like an anxious puppy.

Previous to Shawna, I'd always thought of foreplay as a gateway connecting the sensitive female to the thrusting male. But I couldn't keep my hands off of her.

Nuzzling her neck.

Pushing my face into her hair.

Just the thought of sliding her shirt off sent blood to my unit. I wanted to build a church in her name.

But she'd burn it down.

•

Knocking out some emails, I hear PJ from across the house.

"GEORGIE!"

I go to him, because I can tell he's working. Probably on something for me.

"Give us a look, mate!" He leans his head away from the screen, so I can see. The handout.

"PJ. It's perfect. Seriously."

PJ acts as my unpaid social media director. He makes flyers, draws stuff up, uploads photos and makes sure that the TTTS.org website, Instagram, Twitter and Facebook are all up to date.

I think all of that shit is so stupid; I rarely look at it.

The last time I checked, he'd slid in a photo from one of my classes, boldly centered on a trashy gringa's ass. I was not happy.

"PJ, what the fuck? Bikini shots? Not appropriate."

"No? Not for the Facebook, ay?"

"My mom looks at that!"

"Uhhh, Twittah?"

"No! Not even Twitter!"

"Ah, mate. Lighten up! Twit it and quit it, ay?"

I tried to keep from laughing, but he got me.

To thank him for the flyer, I make a special lunch for us. And of course, I've made extra for the Tsviks. Like a preying animal, PJ smells the seared tuna and potatoes, just as I plate them. He walks in and hands me a USB drive.

"Looks scrumptious!"

I stole the recipe from The Wine Bar in town. Don't tell. It's a favorite spot for expats, and I'm pretty sure PJ knows their old waitress biblically. He shoves in three mouthfuls.

"Not too bad, eh?"

"Mate, on the postah—I emailed yah the PDF. Backup plan. Donny Chi's can be a bit dodgy."

"Great. Smart."

Don Chichos, the hostel with a working commercial printer, is hit and miss. Sometimes using a thumb drive there is like throwing a penny in a well.

"Awesome. Thanks so much for doing that." A piece of tuna drops onto his t-shirt.

"Bugger!"

I hope it doesn't stain. His t-shirt: *Your Tattoo is Stupid.*

I walk a plate down to Tsvika. His door is slightly ajar, so I know he's here.

"Tsviks? Tsvika? I made..."

I use the plate to push open his door. It's empty. It's so rare to see his door open; I can't help myself and look inside. I set the plate on his desk and take a look at his stacks of papers. All topographic maps. A glint of metal catches my eye. I move a few books on his bookshelf and see that it's the topmost bullet in a gun magazine.

What the fuck?

I pick it up, handle it gingerly and conclude that it's a clip for a

Glock 9mm. Honestly, I have no idea, but it's the same color black as Jake Gyllenhaal's gun in *End of Watch* (great movie) and every other gun on earth. Plus, Glock sounds the coolest. I put it back in its place. It's tempting to snoop around more, but hanging out by myself in Tsvika's room is not a good idea.

A gun?

Really?

Fucking weirdo.

●

It's hot. Again. I try to rally in the afternoon, to do the printing, but I decide to take a really quick nap.

Adios two hours.

At dusk, I grab my waterproof flashlight (thanks, mom) and bundle the USB drive into two small Ziplocs, stuffed into three big Ziplocs for the printouts, Russian doll style. You can't be too careful about water—both rain and ocean—on the islands.

I fire up the S.S. Minnow and head into town. Bocas just woke up from its nap, too. Lights flicker on, and music reaches me across the water.

For a tropical slum, it really is beautiful.

I tie up at a friendly dock and head to Don Chichos. As I pass, a thug kid calls out.

"Weed, Weed, Coca?" spoken at the cadence of "Duck, Duck, Goose?" Wouldn't that be such a great t-shirt for PJ?

For all of the hardworking, affable folks trying to build a life here, there's a surplus of idle adolescent males selling drugs, playing with their phones and adding zero value. I'm so tall and recognizable that this salesy chirping has subsided. After saying, "No, gracias." three hundred times, it's nearly stopped. Otherwise, I'd hear it every ten feet. Plus, most of these derelicts know that I work for Raúl. They know better than to mess with anything even remotely related to him— especially scoring drugs for one of his gringo employees.

The power goes out.

Mother…fucker.

I'm only a few feet from Don Chichos, and I see the shadow of their reception guy do what everyone does when the power goes out— lock the door. It could be ten minutes; it could be all night.

I knock.

"Puedo esperar aquí? Necesito la impresora." Somehow, waiting in the dark to use the printer feels completely normal.

"Sí, si quieres. Pero, sin luz." Sin luz means no light. Whether or not there is no power doesn't matter to anyone here. There's simply no light.

"Bueno. Voy a esperar. Quieres cervecita?" Waiting in Bocas is synonymous with drinking beer.

"Oh, sí."

I grab two cold Balboas from the bodega next door, and we sit together on the steps. He asks to see my flashlight and starts taunting insects with it, which brings the bats. Some of the bats are so big here; they prey on small surface fish. Why can't they eat all of the spiders?

I look back across the water toward home.

Maybe PJ's laptop is charged and we can watch one of his movies.

What a waste.

•

The next morning, in the middle of working on my *Esquire* assignment, I do what I have been able to avoid for months. I write Shawna.

From: Georgeous

To: Shawna B.

Subject: greetings from the ghetto paradise

hey—

this is a no reason email. you don't need to respond. i just pulled pj's hair out of the shower drain. i don't know why he always uses my shower, when he has his own. well, other than that mine is ten times cleaner.

anyway, it reminded me of how much yours sheds everywhere. have you ever thought about harvesting half of it for transplants? some rogaine user would pay a pretty penny. and, of course, you'd still be left with a full head of hair.

that was a really lame way of saying that i thought of you, and it made me smile. i just wanted to send some love your way. i hope school is going well (future) dr. shawna.

g

I hate myself for writing her. I do one last proofread of my assignment. By the time I send it off to TR, her response pops up.

From: Shawna B.

To: Georgeous

Subject: RE: greetings from the ghetto paradise

You are such an asshole!

I hate myself for how easy it is for you to charm me with your twisted humor. ASSHOLE.

Regardless, it's nice to hear from you.

XX Shawna

PS I ALWAYS gather up all of my hair from the drain after I shower, so I don't know what you're talking about.

PPS You know you and PJ are textbook co-dependent, right?

PPPS I remember you always thinking and joking via quizzes, but seeing them published online is incredible and horrifying. For example—that last one about smart girls wanting to be called pretty? It's painfully inaccurate. Fuck you.

Señor Helado is back, doing laps on his BMX bike/ice cream stand contraption. His little clown horn is going to give him carpal tunnel. The sound is mind numbing.

The Praúler does not look pleased.

Heepheepheepheepheep. Raúl is hammering up the *Ladies' Night* sign, trying to attract the gringas. Señor Helado cruises by for the THIRD time. Raúl sets the sign down and calmly walks out to the street. He whistles, and Señor Helado pedals over, ecstatic for a sale in the oppressive heat. Please note: Señor Helado's profit on this transaction is twenty cents, max. These guys live on $2-3 a day.

"Qué tipo de…" What flavor do you want?

Hammer in hand, Raúl cocks back and starts beating the shit out of the horn. After fifteen swings (the sound of metal on metal is horrific), the handlebars bend and the horn finally breaks loose. Mr. Ice Cream takes the whole thing somberly. He sits back on the edge of the bike seat, just far enough away to avoid the blows, keeping his eyes safely away from Raúl's.

Raúl finishes, turns and walks back into the bar. He looks at the *Ladies Night* sign and turns to me for the tape measure.

I should be scared, but I'm not. We're four doors down from the police station, and there's absolutely zero chance of this bludgeoning getting reported, even if it had been witnessed firsthand by officers.

My heart goes out to Señor Helado. But goddamn if I'm not glad to have the honking gone.

"Estás listo, para su clase? De Turbo?" Are you ready for your swim class? In Turbo?

I got PJ to repurpose our flyer for my next class, in Turbo, Colombia. Is that not the coolest name for a city?

And Raúl is going to drive me.

•

One of the French expats in Bocas opened up Hotel Almar Capurgana in Turbo about six months ago. We'd been drinking and chatting at La Barracuda (the restaurant, not the swim class) one night, and I was on my soapbox about how the majority of people living near waterways in developing countries can't swim. It's a crime. I'm pretty sure most of the boat-taxi drivers in Bocas can't swim.

Michel seconded my statement by telling me a story about a small open-air boat sinking after a monsoon. The quick burst of rain here will nearly rip the shirt off your back. It'll fill a small boat in thirty seconds. We keep a plastic iced tea pitcher in the Minnow, for this exact reason. It went down just a few hundred feet from a Bocas dock. The driver didn't make it. He was returning empty beer bottles from Bastimientos. A capsized boat and a dead man, all for $9 worth of recycling.

"Eeef you would liiike to have one of your classes in Turbo, teeell me, and you can use our pool, eh?"

"Really?"

"But of cooourse? Even zee Colombian kids need swim, no?"

"That would be amazing. I could even combo it with a visa renewal trip. I'm so tired of going to Puerto Viejo."

"But why? Zee backpacker girls in Costa Rica are quite beautiful, no?"

"True. As long as you pack penicillin for the STDs."

"Ah ha! Oui oui. Zees are not zee girls you take to your motheeerh."

Ooof.

I need to write my mom.

•

Raúl says that he has family in Medellín. I do believe him, because his family is constantly arriving from all over to stay with him. But I can't help but suspect that he has some other, more clandestine purpose for our trip.

At first, when I mentioned taking a few days off to go to Colombia, I was shocked that Raúl offered to drive me. I was blown away and almost touched—thinking that it was a thank you for taking care of the bar. But now that he's asked if I'm "listo" about five times, the offer doesn't seem so generous.

It's like when you ask your dad to play catch with you, but he's always too busy. Then, one weekend, he starts hounding you, "Wanna play catch? Come on! Let's go!" But it's only because he got caught shagging his secretary.

A smarter person would decline Raúl's offer.

But there's no way I'm turning down a free ride in his top-of-the-line Land Cruiser Prado. And what better for his shady business trip than a smiling white dude saying, "Hola! I'm here to teach the kids to swim! Look! I brought goggles and water-wings!"

From: Shawna B.

To: Georgeous

Subject: RE: RE: greetings from the ghetto paradise

I have been drinking…so hopefully I'll wait until the morning to send this.

Do you miss me? I'm curious. I think about you all the time. And I wanted to say I'm sorry. I should have written you months ago. I don't know why I am/was always so hard on you. And it was mean to say you were, "So fucking lost, it's pathetic."

God, just thinking of those words coming out of my mouth makes me feel like the biggest bitch. I do think you are searching, and I think that is a good thing. And it is so great what you do with the kids. I kind of stalk your Teach Them To Swim Facebook page. I giggle at all of the excited kids and always check the counter. You have taught 57 kids to swim! That is so great, George! That is more than most people do in a lifetime.

Anyway. I'm sorry.

I miss you. I really do.

Your biggest fan.

XX Shawna

PS More pictures with you with your shirt off on Facebook, please?

Shawna was smart not to email sooner. It gave me a chance to miss her. Most females are much too impatient to wait. They need to know how you feel about them RIGHT NOW. But not Shawna. She's no dummy. And I'm glad she felt bad. Because I pretty much hated her when I left.

She cheated on me.

And I still let her come visit me. Here. In the place I came to escape her.

From: Georgeous

To: Shawna B.

Subject: good morning sunshine!

…liquor is my best friend and severest critic…

no, not you. that's hemingway. he always was tight with the bottle.

big night, eh?

you really miss me? seriously? i miss you too. as the song, says: you're my favorite mistake.

ok. that was a little biting. but you deserve it. to prove to you that i still think about you, last week i finally used your first aid kit. it made me start thinking about you. then i got hard, came robustly to your image and dropped a perfect air jordan semen outline on my stomach. how march madness is that?

i gotta go pack for colombia.

love,

the guy that spanks to you (and misses you too)

ps i'm very flattered that you read my prolific 40 words of love advice. some are fiction. some are fantasy. some are inspired by pj or my bar patrons. but you're right—most are just lines that are supposed to be funny and definitely supposed to get me paid.

PJ drops me off at The Wreck Deck early, with his board in the Minnow. He's capitalizing on the 6:30am alarm to grab some waves at Playa Ponch.

"Thanks so much, PJ."

"No worries, mate! Say g'day to Pablo for us, ay?" He's been all over the Pablo Escobar jokes for days, and he wouldn't say no to a small bag of blow. But he knows I'm too timid and law abiding to dabble in micro-smuggling.

PJ's t-shirt: *Sorry I'm late. Your mom got a flat tire.*

Raúl is chatting with his "Primo," who is coming with us. Cousin or not, the guy is a beast. And he's driving. This surprises me, as I've never seen Raúl hand over the keys to his precious Prado to anyone.

But I realize if we get carjacked, Primo would be the first to get shot.

Well played, Raúl.

Primo is so damn thick; I'd almost feel sorry for the bullet.

I'm thankful for the backseat. We've got a full day of travel ahead of us, and I really don't want to make small talk with Raúl.

•

You could drive the thirty thousand miles of roads connecting Alaska to the southernmost tip of Chile, if it weren't for Panama and Colombia ruining it. A sixty-mile stretch on their border is the only portion of the Americas that has a gap in the Pan-American Highway. It's called the Darién Gap. Although it sounds like Damien and Devin's older Spanish brother that needs braces, it's a swampy, lawless land and full of thieves, drug traffickers, military separatists and hostage-takers—all often one in the same.

The Darién Gap is the main reason I opted to hop in with Raúl. We'll still need to take two ferries, three major freeways and a cargo boat to get there, but at least I know we'll get there.

•

After twenty hours of travel and three water crossings, we get our passports stamped in Colombia. The bumpy roads, fatigue and air conditioning lull me into a low grade nap.

I wake up, a few hours later, to a makeshift roadblock. It's not what I had pictured from the weekend I spent binge-watching *Locked Up Abroad*. I do NOT recommend doing this, the month before you move to Central America.

Stoic does not describe how chill Raúl and Primo are. Three paramilitary guys stand in front of a single log that they've used to block the road. It would destroy the Land Cruiser, if we were to make a run for it. Their weapons are a little mismatchy: machete, revolver and submachine gun. We sit in a standoff for ages.

Maybe thirty seconds.

The guy in charge (the one with the machine gun) walks up to the window. Primo does not roll it down. It's counterintuitive. My first instinct would be to roll down the window and say, "Hola guys! Who wants a piece of gum?"

Another thirty-second standoff. Maybe the Land Cruiser Prado has bulletproof glass?

You'd think that Raúl would have made me get out of the car, while yelling out the window, "Take the white dude for ransom, but make it quick—we need to roll." But I'm not even part of the equation.

Phew.

Mr. Big Gun taps the window—but lightly. He adds a nod to kick off some dialogue. Primo cracks it 1/4th of an inch. They have the briefest conversation, and it's impossible to understand them, but this is what I hear in my head:

"Dude, my boss owns this road. Why are you here? Nice truck, by the way. Leather? Sweet."

"What do you think, we're stupid? We're having dinner with your boss tonight. If you don't move that fucking log, I'm going to stick that gun up your ass."

Raúl is cleaning his fingernails with a pocketknife, like a mother-in-law filing her nails. I'd kill to take his blood pressure.

Not. Concerned. At. All.

"Hmmm. That sounds plausible. But how do I know if it's true? Wow, your forearms are bigger than our pathetic roadblock. So, you use mostly free weights or what?"

"I can smell the roasting goat from here, and his wife is making her famous tomatillo sauce. Later, we smoke cigars and fuck whores. Hopefully one of them is your sister."

Nice rip, Primo.

"Tomatillo sauce? Why didn't you say so! Please go ahead! Welcome to Colombia!"

•

Primo and Raúl drop me off in Turbo. They're heading toward Raúl's family's place in Medellín. A globally noteworthy town, thanks to *Entourage* and *Narcos*. If it weren't for Netflix, how would anyone learn geography?

Michel's place is flawless. A bunch of simple bungalows surrounding a pool, just steps from the ocean—the whole place just smells clean. But, like Bocas, when you step outside the immaculate hotel compound, there's endless plastic trash, unfinished housing projects and decrepit vehicles.

I take a dip in the swimming pool. It feels so luxurious—I almost can't stand it. Toweling off, I ask the lobby attendant if I can use their little computer kiosk. They've already printed PJ's flyer and posted it at the front desk. A rare, yet splendid taste of efficiency.

I should be good on the *Esquire* work, but I like to check in daily, in case something comes up. It's too sweet of a gig not to stay on top of it.

All I see are two emails from Shawna. She's like a bad habit. You won't do it for months. Then overnight, you're back to smoking a pack a day.

I'd be lying if I didn't admit that it's nice to see her name.

From: Shawna B.
To: Georgeous
Subject: Air Jordan
Speechless.

Other than the fact that Shawna fucked her UCLA research partner while we were dating, we also broke up because Shawna is such a wild card. You'd joke about sex with a nun, and she'd laugh hysterically. She'd even add her own twist: "Who cleans the rosary beads after?" Gross. The next day, you might take a jab at a barista that was a little righteous with the foam and say he has Asperger's. She'd snap, "You are so judgey! Autism is an epidemic! You're probably on the spectrum yourself!" So mean. And so right.

Recalling this, I'm scared to open her second email.

From: Shawna B.
To: Georgeous
Subject: Did you seriously not take a picture?

Wow. That is incredible. I would like to have seen it. And I'm so flattered to be the inspiration!

Just thinking of you touching your dick while thinking about me made me so…well, let's just say I had to go and change my underwear. I know how much you hate it when I say dick. So dick dick dick dick dick!

Be careful in Colombia, OK? I hear skinny white boys are their favorite appetizer.

XX

Shawna

PS I'm so glad you finally used the first aid kit!

Hearing her talk about getting wet instantly turns me on. Plus, I'm glad I'm not in trouble. If it weren't for the reception guy, I might snap one off right here.

Up in my room, I open the mini-fridge. It's stocked with beer and a note:

Monsieur George—

Welcome! So wonderful what you are doing with the children! Enjoy a few drinks on me. Sorry to have missed you. Looking forward to seeing you when I return to Bocas.

Bon voyage,

Michel

Free bungalow. Free use of the pool. Stocked fridge. All this from a

guy I really only hung out with one night. Crazy. I feel blessed. I walk
out on the front steps, drink in the twilight and replay the long day.

Finally it hits me.

That roadblock could have gone so, so badly. If I had been with
anyone other than Raúl, I would be sleeping on the ground in the
jungle right now, guarded by well-armed nineteen-year-olds. A phone
call would've been placed to the embassy, and then my mother would
be contacted. This would be followed by a lot of waiting, a few
beatings and a standoff. My mom would mortgage the house for the
ransom, and I'd be returned thirty pounds lighter and never quite the
same. And that's the best-case scenario—where my last cardio workout
doesn't involve me digging my own grave.

My heart starts to race. I pound my beer. It doesn't help. I start
bugging out and lay on the bed. I calm myself the only way I can think
of: by taking my pants off.

I think of Vanesa and Camila and get liftoff, but that's it. I swap
Camila out for Shawna.

It works.

Sometimes we'd be on the couch, and I'd accidentally get turned
on—probably from smelling her. Nonchalantly, Shawna would turn
around, inquisitive.

"Oh! Do you have a present for me?"

"Indeed?"

"Thank you!" She'd grab at me, and I'd resist. But barely.

"Let's go in the bedroom. I want to be inside…"

"Later. For now, just be selfish, OK?" She'd put me in her mouth and tie her hair up simultaneously. It was the hottest thing I've ever seen.

But right now, all I can think of is her with that other dude's hands on her. The guy that put the *ruin* in the UCLA Bruins.

I give up, put shorts on, open another beer and walk outside.

•

I wake up early, disoriented in my room. The sunrise is stunning. I start prepping for class, but I still have three hours before 10am. Laying out all of the gear only burns eight minutes. Normally, I wouldn't leave anything anywhere, but the hotel has enough security to start a small army. One security guard sits by the empty pool, half watching me, half asleep.

I ask him to watch my stuff, so I can grab some breakfast.

"Sí, sí. Ve a comer. Todo bien." No worries. I'll watch it. Go eat.

Everyone here is so nice; it's unsettling.

The reception dude greets me. Did he work all night?

"Algo para comer, Señor Lewis?" (sounds like Looouueees).

"Sí, por favor. Gracias."

The spread is insane. It's nice not to cook for once. PJ is probably back on his diet of Captain Crunch (yes, they sell Los Crunchberries in Bocas) and beers at 10:30am.

I wish PJ were here to take photos. But he and Raúl don't mix. Certainly not on a trip like this.

Eggs, fresh fruit, fried plantains. I take it all down. Delicious. I ask for the bill, and the reception guy (also doubles as the buffet guy) says no.

His orders from Michel are firm: take no money from the gringo. I slip him a ten, and he declines.

"Pues no. Tú eres el instructor!"

But I insist.

"Por favooor." He reluctantly pockets it. I'm relieved. But I'm not ecstatic about our worker/patron relationship. The randomness of disparity is such a mindfuck.

I try to stoke him out with what every tourist should attempt: humility and appreciation. It's not nearly enough, but it makes me feel better.

"Mil gracias por todo, amigo. La piscina, especialmente." Thank you so much for everything—especially the pool.

"Aye, por nada. Gracias a ti." His graciousness makes me want to buy him a car.

At 9:40am, they start coming. And coming. Ten moms, eighteen kids and five babes-in-arms. I hope I don't have to explain, in Spanish, that I don't teach babies. In all likelihood, one of these kids is the offspring of the gun-toting road blockers.

Bummer I didn't think to offer them a flyer.

This class is huge, but it's not my biggest yet. The pool security guard gives me a *you're fucked, bro* glance. I decide to divide and conquer.

Everyone looks timid, so I invite three of the larger kids in—all about ten years old. One of the little boys gets so excited, he drops a fully intact turd into the pool. I try not to laugh. The security guard shakes his head. Not his problem.

Like lightning, a mom opens her large canvas shopping bag/South

American purse and whips out a plastic bag. She could've found three hundred of them littering the streets, just outside the hotel.

Scoop, twist, tie, gone.

We quarantine the pool for twenty seconds, and the kids jump right back in. This isn't *Caddy Shack*. No one freaks out. If you're afraid of swimming with a little feces, then you shouldn't spend time in the water down here.

I start to realize that no one cares about the swim lessons. They just want to spend a day at a hotel pool.

Fine by me.

I hand out the goggles. The kids are suspicious. Gringos don't give away stuff for free.

A little girl tugs at my arm. Her mom speaks for her.

"Mi hija está fascinada con los Juegos Olímpicos. Está enamorada de Miguel Felpas." My daughter is fascinated with the Olympics. Her favorite is…

"Michael Phelps?"

"Sí, sí! El campeón! Ella estudió los ejercicios." Mom illustrates by showing me the backstroke.

The little girl looks at me. Without uttering a word, she projects: *I came here to crush it today, Mister.*

"Como te llamas?"

"Elisa."

"Aye, qué bonita! Te gustas los Juegos Olimpicos, eh?"

She looks at her mom for encouragement. Her mom's got her back. Her mom's eyes turn toward me, with expectations. Make it happen, homeboy.

"Sí, quiero ir a los Juegos Olímpicos y competir." She wants to compete in the Olympics. And she's going to start training—today.

Like an Airborne Ranger, she puts on her goggles and slides in. It's awful. She looks like she's going to drown. BUT, she can decently mimic freestyle, breaststroke and backstroke. She may have sprinkled in a butterfly, but she was standing in the shallow end, so it's hard to say. She learned all of this from watching TV. Incredible.

"Muy, muy bueno. Un par de cosas, OK?" Great job. Just a few things.

She looks at me, like I'm Obi Wan Kenobi. I show her how to keep her head down, to kick more rhythmically and to glide in between strokes.

The rest of the hotel pool is a splash-fest, but Elisa doesn't mind. Within twenty minutes, she can stay afloat and cross the narrow end by herself.

"Estás listo para el siguiente paso?" We're moving onto the next step, but it's a big step.

"Sí." If I'd asked her to swim the English Channel, she would have given the same answer. This girl is all business.

Breathing on your side is really tough to teach kids (adults, too), because the muscles in your neck are prewired to arch straight back when you need oxygen—for survival. I try all of my tricks, but it doesn't stick. It took Damien three weeks to get it. But Elisa wants a crash course, and I want to deliver.

I pick her up and sit her next to her mom, who is dangling her feet in the water.

"Practicar aquí, OK?"

"En la piscina!" She wants to do it IN the pool. Feisty little one.

"Cien veces aquí." One hundred dry practice runs, then we try it in the pool. Her mom, like Rocky's coach Mickey, accepts this negotiation.

Stroke, chin, shoulder, breathe, repeat. I make her touch her chin to her shoulder, which is overkill, but it's working. Her mom follows and keeps her focused.

"Hija! El mentón!" The chin! I hope they invite me over for dinner, so her mom can tell me, authoritatively, what to do with my life.

97, 98, 99, bingo.

She jumps back into the pool and dominates. She swims the full length and back, hammering her stroke through the useless boys in her path. Hitting the wall next to us, she gasps for breath and turns to us for validation.

"Perfecto!"

Her mom pats me on the shoulder, and Elisa breaks with a big proud smile. Turn the Facebook counter to 58.

•

After two more days of lounging, I write Michel a thank you note and check out. Primo and Raúl roll up. They both hop out and throw down some monster bro hugs—they're so happy to see me!

Just kidding.

They stay in the car and don't even nod hello. I reach for the cargo latch above the rear door, and Primo barks from his seat.

"NO."

I keep my backpack with me in the backseat. I wait until we've been on the road for ten minutes and casually look over my shoulder. There's a wooden box in the back, about the size of a coffin for a caiman or a small alligator. It probably contains the same amount of bite, if it's what I think it is.

•

At the border, we get stopped. Primo pulls slightly forward of the guard and rolls down MY window for me. Thanks, homie.

"El propósito de su visita?" The purpose of your visit? I hand him my passport, along with my Certified Red Cross Swim Instructor card clipped above my photo. This little piece of laminated paper comes in handy.

"Instrucción de nadar, en Turbo." The guard hesitates for a moment. I unfold a flyer from my bag and hand it to him.

Legit.

A stoic nod and we're on our way.

Now I know why Raúl was so adamant about giving me a "free ride." He just turned me into a drug mule. Raúl puts the kilo in kilometer.

My eyes burn a hole through the back of his headrest for an hour.

I'm mad but only at myself. I saw this coming a mile away.

The box behind me could hold at least a dozen kilos of coke. I just whored myself out to deliver two hundred bucks worth of goggles and create one additional swimmer on earth—cute little Elisa.

I feel so dirty—I want to take a shower. I think about business cards printed up that say: *George Lewis—Non-profit CEO/Drug Trafficker.* But even in the self-loathing, I can't keep my eyes open. The Land Cruiser is that comfy.

I lie across the backseat, catch a few glances of the lush jungle and doze.

4

How to deliver compliments and flowers:

When you give your girl something, do it in public. Especially in front of your mutual friends. Women are social beings. And the experience of receiving attention is just as important as the attention itself. If you're gonna drop $100 on flowers, have them sent to her workplace for everyone to see.

It's bittersweet to have eighty-nine days left on this new visa. Every single time I cross the border to get it renewed, I think, "This will be the last time I have to do this. There's no way I'll still be in Bocas in ninety days." Soon enough, *Kahchunk* goes the passport stamp. Three more months…gone.

Damn, it feels good be back in my own bed. How is it possible to be tired after dozing all day? Sure, it was in the backseat, and we did traverse a small country. But, basically, I slept all day.

Fitful post-sojourn sleep.

•

Making coffee in the morning, I hear a boat approaching. It's the
DHL guy. Jesus, Tsvika gets a lot of expedited mail. I walk out to our
little dock—saving him from having to disembark. Signing for it, it's
the thinnest envelope in the world. They couldn't have just emailed
this?

I hear movement on the path in front of our house. It's Marquito
sitting tandem on a bike with an older kid. He's riding on a makeshift
wooden seat that fits in between the actual seat and the handlebars. I've
seen a few of these, and they're a clever use of a skill saw. It's one of
those things where the handmade version is ten times more effective
than anything that could be designed commercially. It's like how an
airplane boarding-pass makes a better bookmark than an actual
bookmark.

Marquito sees me and jumps off the bike.

"Marquito. Quieres un chocolate?"

"Sí, si quieres." Yeah, if you don't mind making it. What kid is
polite about chocolate milk?

"Venga."

We have Quik, mostly for PJ, but Marquito gets his share. Little
Marco often does a drive-by the house mid-morning. It's quiet on Isla
Carenero, and he knows now is when I'm most likely to go for a swim,
to cool off. But I also suspect that he's lonely. Like most kids of single
parents, he seeks companionship. Someone to witness his life.

With Marco preoccupied with the chocolate milk, it's safe to run the DHL down to Tsvika.

Now that I know that Tsvika's got an armory in his room, I've been avoiding coming down here. I knock, wait a few seconds and then open his door.

Setting the envelope on his desk, I do a quick scan. Everything looks the same, but the gun magazine is gone.

And...

There's a folder.

Fuck it.

I slide it off his bookshelf, noting its position, so I can return it without causing suspicion. It's full of 8x10 glossy photos.

The first one?

It's of me.

I flip through the rest.

The next one is also of me, but I'm talking to Raúl, at The Wreck. The next thirteen are all of Raúl. The last two are clearly from our trip to Colombia.

Tsvika, you can cook your own breakfast, creeper.

Leaving Marco alone for more than two minutes is not an option. I replace the folder and head back upstairs.

I need to knock out some work on the computer—so I refresh our drinks and let him sit with me in my room. I look down at Marquito, but my eyes go right through him. I'm babysitting the son of my drug lord boss, who is under surveillance by my roommate. My other roommate's biggest concern is that his favorite condoms are out of stock at the bodega.

Perfect.

I toss Marco some pens and paper. He knows I won't tolerate him destroying shit in the house. But he gets me back by drawing knives, bombs and mutilation.

From: Rogers, Timothy

To: Georgeous

Subject: Slightly quicker turnaround

Attachment: EsquisiteSavage16.doc

George—

All is well here Stateside, thank you for asking.

We seem to have more work than we can handle.

If you ever plan to return, do let me know.

Two small things:

1. As I had mentioned, we're on a little tighter schedule this week. If you could turn this around quickly, it would be greatly appreciated.

2. Do let me know that your paychecks are being deposited? Accounting told me that there was a snafu last time with the wire. It's certainly not a huge amount of money, but it likely goes a long way there, in the land of the Panama Hat.

Best,

TR

PS I enjoyed your last advice piece about having flowers delivered at work, etc.

How can I keep him as my nemesis, when he's so nice? I loosen up with a response to Shawna. Thank god Marquito can't read English.

From: Georgeous

To: Shawna B.

Subject: colomboner

you know i love it when you talk dirty. i've never met a female who uses the words pussy and dick so conversationally. bravo.

colombia was insane. it makes bocas look "not that poor," which says a lot.

how's school?

xio (kisses, boners & hugs)

g

ps does my cavalier dick-mentioning sound forced? it is.

pps one of my little swim students is here with me. otherwise, i might try to nude skype with you. you know, for old time's sake ;)

I rip through the assignment. It's painful to have to read it on the screen, but they're pretty short. Dan must have a new copy editor that's somebody's cousin, because I find two gerunds and a comma splice. First I think it's sloppy. Then I'm glad that I can offer some value, because I really need that $400 a month. I reread Dan's article aloud, and Marco listens. But as soon as he doesn't hear, "Marquito—do you wanna go swimming?" he goes back to drawing a tank.

Shawna has already written me back.

From: Shawna B.

To: Georgeous

Subject: Your dick

That's not entirely true. I say penis…sometimes. But if it is yours, and I'm sucking it, it's called a dick. Dick dick dick dick!

School is horrible. Why did I stay at UCLA this whole time? Every time I think of how smart I was to go the easy route and keep the same advisor from M.A. to Ph.D., I drive through Brentwood and want to kill myself. If they import one more douchey guy here, I may escape to our homeland. I can't believe I actually miss Pasadena.

Are you ever coming home? I used to think you were on a really, really long vacation (and, more likely, trying to get away from me), but now I'm starting to wonder…

X 3 > O

Shawna

PS That sign off was: Kisses, Titties, Pussies & Hugs.

From: Georgeous

To: Rogers, Timothy

Subject: On time on budget

Attachments: EsquisiteSavage16_GL_clean.doc, EsquisiteSavageLove16_GL_markups.doc

TR—

You are too kind to me, and I don't deserve it.

Regardless, thank you. I may take you up on it someday.

Regarding work: I made quite a few edits on this one (i.e. about three times more than normal). I've attached both the clean and redlined versions. I'm not sure if you care, but it would appear that Dan might have a new copy editor? Anyway, if you have any problems or want me to re-review it, I'm more than happy to.

George

PS I absolutely received my salary, and thank you for the bonus. You overpay me to write bad love advice, but please do keep the checks coming.

I put the computer to sleep. It's time to take Marquito for a swim.

•

Banco Nacional is the only bank in town. I'm in line with a few of the local shop owners, waiting for it to open. They run out of cash quickly. I am probably the only person here putting money into the bank. A pretty hot, tanned tourist tries the ATM, fails and gets in line behind me.

"Do you know what the deal is?" Her smile. Wow.

"Ha. It's a joke. They run out of money every day. Every single day. My favorite part of coming here is watching the expats walk up and ask, 'Does the ATM have money today?'"

"That's awful. But funny, too!"

"It's like someone asking, 'Does the pharmacy have medicine?' But what do you expect? It's fucking Bocas."

"It IS fucking Bocas! Hi! I'm Andrea!"

"George. Nice to meet you. Cool shirt!" It says: *Drugs—the only way to get the U.S. to adopt the metric system.*

"Yeah, it's a lie. I'm terrible at math. I just liked the defiance of it."

"Defiance. Nice word choice. My roommate may try to steal that shirt from you. Or sleep with you. Or both."

"I'll stay on the lookout. Is he as tall as you? And wait, roommate? You LIVE here?"

"Yeah. Sort of. I've been here almost ten months now. It goes by quick. I work at Barco Hundido. And no, he's not as tall. But he is handsome and charming."

"But you are handsome and charming...so...he's a shorter version of you?"

Touché, attractive tourist.

"Uhhh..."

"And you work at The Wreck Deck? I read about that place in the Lonely Planet. We are for sure going there." The doors open, the line has grown and we move forward by one person.

"Well say hello if you do. I work tonight and tomorrow night."

"Definitely. So, how long is this gonna take?"

"To manually extract cash from the human teller? Probably half an hour. Settle in."

"Damn. OK. 'Island time,' right? Who says 'teller' anyway?"

"Losers and old people? But don't you think it's weird that 'ATM' is its own word now? No one thinks of it as an acronym for Automated Teller Machine."

"Huh. Yeah. It's kinda like skyscraper. You don't really think about a building scraping the sky; you just hear the word and know what it means."

"Lexicon puns? Are you sure you're in the right place?"

"Back atchya." She beams. I look at her thin, toned arms.

"So, are you a climber?"

"Yeah. How'd you know?"

"Your arms."

"Oh, here we go. 'You're so muscular for a girl.' And then they go talk to my girlfriend."

"I wasn't saying that..."

"That's what it sounded like. It's not a big deal, I hear it all the time."

"I like how strong you are. That's it."

"Thank you. Most guys don't like girls with callouses on their hands." She shows me.

"Idiots."

One more person moves forward in line. At this speed, our banter will get awkward shortly. I need to tap into my work skills.

The key to tending bar is being a good conversationalist—to get people to talk about themselves. The key to getting people to talk to themselves is to ask them easy questions. Bad example: "What's new?" What if nothing is new? Good example: "Do you always drink beer?" Bad example: "What's your favorite book?" What if they hate reading? Good example: "How long have you been in Panama?" I turn back around and throw her a few softballs.

"How long are you here for?"

"In Bocas? Just a week."

"Wow, short trip."

"Yeeeah…we also wanted to spend some time in Panama City and maybe Boquette. But now I wish we were staying here the whole time."

Me too.

"Where are you from?"

"Portland. You?"

"Outside of LA. Do you know Pasadena?"

"LA? Yuck."

"Hey! Don't hate on LA. I've been to Portland, and ordering a coffee there is like asking to marry someone's daughter."

"Whoa! I run one of those coffee shops."

"Which one?"

"Stumptown."

"In the Ace Hotel?"

"Yeah! How'd you…"

"My friend in New York goes to the one there."

"Wow. Small world. And sorry, I'm sure Passy Dina is nice."

"How many people call you Portlandrea? After the TV show?"

"Everyone."

"Sorry. Not very clever. And I was trying to impress you with my wit."

"HA! At least you tried! You're already impressing me, by being funny and looking me in the eyes." She's right.

"Hey, I'm up next. I have time to burn before work. Why don't you go ahead of me, and maybe I'll see you at The Wreck sometime while you're here?"

"That is so nice. Deal!"

She steps in front of me without hesitation, knowing that her butt is worthy of its own hip hop song.

•

The Wreck is packed. When you buy a bar in the Tropics, don't go overkill investing in music. A few playlists sprinkled with Bob Marley and you're golden.

When it gets busy, I've got to manage my time. It's all about volume. If someone asks for two gin rammalammadingdongs shaken with a twist, I fake a, "What?" and open two Balboas. They'll protest, briefly, but as soon as their hands touch the ice-cold bottles, it's over, and I just saved ten minutes.

No tip? Next time, they get Soberanas.

By midnight, it's spring break gone wild at The Wreck. Gringo females dance on the bar tops, and shady local creepers wait to catch them when they fall. My neck is sore from turning to look at the door for Andrea.

We hit a lull. The DJ spices it up. I hand out a few free shots to some locals. Nightspots in Bocas are fickle. We could sell five grand one night and be dead the next. To combat this, Raúl hired a DJ on weekends. I thought my dated iPod with a cracked screen was fine, but he was right. A good DJ can be hypnotic. It's risky though, because two bogey songs in a row and the crowd will move to another bar.

A white dude walks up, after just exchanging cash with one of the most notorious stolen goods salesman at The Wreck. The thief is a nice guy and tips well, but asking every gringo if he wants to buy a stolen camera kills the ambiance.

"Can I get a rum and Coke?"

"Sure. What'd you buy?" I fix his drink.

"Huh?"

"I work here, dude. Camera or iPhone?"

Busted.

"iPhone. I know it's lame, but mine got stolen yesterday…"

"No need to explain, man. It's fucking Bocas. Drink is on the house."

"Hey! Thanks, man! I'm Kevin."

"George. Have fun."

I don't even bother remembering their names, until I've seen them around for a few weeks.

"Hey, do you have any good food recommendations?"

"Sure. Do you have a girl?"

"Yeah! We just got engaged!"

"Congrats. In town? If she likes low key and tasty, check out Bocart. If you want a little adventure, take her to dinner at The Firefly on Bastimientos. You have to take a boat and walk a little, but it's worth it. Romantic, and the food is to die for."

"Cool!"

"They speak an English Creole on Basti. If you ask a local, and listen carefully, you'll find it."

"Thanks, bro!"

The mini boat ride and five minute walk to The Firefly is like everything else around here—it's an artificial hardship. You go to dinner via boat, why? Because you want to feel like an explorer, even if it's only for fifteen minutes. It's the same reason hardcore yuppies climb Everest—because their everyday lives are dull and easy. You don't see any farmers climbing mountains or doing triathlons. Because they have real jobs—jobs that are hard.

I see Andrea! She is backpacker-dressed-up, which means a light top, necklace and a pair of shorts.

"HI!"

"Hey, you made it!"

"We were just at Aqua. It was…"

"Fantastic yet disgusting?"

"Yes!"

"My roommate is there. The combination of rapey locals, lusting expats and never ending sea of fresh backpacker girls is…"

"Why we left."

"But, it can be fun sometimes. I'm not gonna lie."

"I know! We spent three hours there. Any bar that has a swing set, a trampoline AND a saltwater pool? I'm IN. No matter how young the crowd is."

"100% agreed. Drink?"

"I'd love a beer. Whatever you recommend. As cold as possible." She wipes the sweat off her brow. I want to lick her fingers. I'm hoping we can have a keg at our wedding. I pop two Balboa bottles.

"Cheers."

"You can drink at work?"

"Only on special occasions." I take a sip and drink her in. Then, I go into a trance for ten seconds.

Comparing her to Shawna.

Mistake.

"Hey, dude?"

Whoops.

A pack of impatient bros seeks my attention. I try to determine whether their moustaches are ironic or if they are part of the visiting U.S. Coast Guard crew, docked nearby. Impossible to tell the difference.

"Sorry guys, what's up?" Like Clint Eastwood in *A Fistful of Dollars*, I holster a Jägermeister bottle.

"Yeah bro, um three Jäger bombs…"

Called it.

"MAAATE!" PJ arrives, drops his drunk elbows on the bar and the three bros mad-dog glare at him. I visualize PJ knocking their teeth out.

"Dude! You are out of Miller Light?"

Miller Light and Coors Light are huge sellers at The Wreck. Need I describe our clientele?

PJ chimes in.

"Nice mo', mate!" This is how PJ says, *I wanna put you in the hospital.* Normally his next alpha male move is to say, "So, you can grow hair on yah lip? That must mean you're a cunt!" Then the blows start flying. I love his protective brotherly vibe, but if he gets in one more fight here, Raúl is gonna…well it's gonna be no bueno. I offer the bros three lukewarm Panamas, hand PJ an icy Balboa from my secret stash and redirect his energy.

"PJ, can you go chill with my friend, Andrea?" I motion toward the end of the bar. She's stayed there, so I know that I have a chance. PJ sees her and shifts gears like a Formula 1 driver. He's an epic wingman. I wipe down the bar pointlessly and watch PJ go to work.

"Aaandreeayuh?"

"Yeah?"

"I'm Georgie's mate! Give us a hug, ay!" He picks her up. It startles her but just for a second.

"Oh, you're his roommate?"

"Yeah! I'm PJ!" I look over and see her checking out his body. Ugh.

But she's just reading his t-shirt: *DIE YUPPIE SCUM! Oh, Wait, That's Me.* And they start hitting it off. I walk a few steps closer to them and hear her say what three out of five women on the island say to him.

"Does anyone ever say you look like Heath Ledger?" Please note: she did not say he looked like a bus driver she knows. Saying you look like someone famous is just a subtler way of saying you're very attractive.

"Really? He was a legend! May he rest in peace." PJ toasts the sky with his beer.

Their new friendship needs some time to marinate, so I head to the back to restock beer. Raúl has enough security guys standing around that there is absolutely zero risk of a super bro jumping behind the bar without getting his nose broken.

We're completely out of cold Panama bottles. We always have backup cans, but the bottles sell faster. And, for some reason, people litter bottles into the water less. The warm bottles won't be cold and servable for another hour.

I head to the dry storage. When I open the door, I see the edge of a blanket catch the wind. It's covering something on the top back shelf.

Unusual.

Curious, I step up on the cases of Panama (trust me, Balboa is way tastier) and lift the blanket. It's so hot, who even owns a blanket in Bocas?

Holy shit.

It's the sketchy box from the Land Cruiser that Primo didn't want me to see. I cover it back up.

Walking back out to the bar, I ice half my load, nod to a monster security guy to cover me and come back. I'm probably safe for two minutes. I pull the box down and open it, curious to witness drug smuggling firsthand. I wonder what they use? Ziplocs? Saran Wrap?

The box is filled with fibrous packing. I dig through it to unveil…the most gigantic gun I have ever seen in my life. Full-blown Rambo-style weapon of death. OK, I have no idea, but it's massive and black, and it's got a gang of bullets loaded in magazines packed into the bottom of the box.

What the fuck?

I try to reconstruct its packing and blanket snuggieness. Raúl *and* Tsvika? Both fully armed? Is the NRA starting a chapter here or what? My mind flashes back to the surveillance photos, and my brain starts spinning.

I walk back to the bar. PJ has Andrea in hysterics. God knows where her friends are. He's holding her over the bannister of The Wreck, clearly telling a story about me.

"He's a LEGEND!"

PJ, you're the best.

Raúl walks in, checks in with his security homies and then walks over to me. Does he know that I saw the assault rifle? But he looks happy, which just means not pissed, and gives me a shoulder tap.

"Tan ocupado, no? Todo bien?" It's busy. I'm making money. Is anything fucked up?

"Sí, sí. La Panama fria está listo. Pero todo bien." We're low on cold beer, but everything else is fine. He finds my answer sufficient and turns his gaze toward PJ. Thank god PJ is not chatting up one of the local girls. PJ hitting on Panamanian females is one of The Praúler's deepest displeasures, besides losing money.

Andrea gasps.

PJ reaches, swipes the air and almost falls in.

I can see that her necklace is gone. And they're searching for it. Andrea runs over to me.

"My necklace! It slipped off! It was my grandmother's! I was so stupid to bring it here!"

She's tough. But the tears come. PJ runs up.

"Mate! Her neckie dropped! But I think I might see where it went, ay? Have you got a set of specs?" Of course I have fucking goggles. But swimming near The Wreck to Raúl is like asking to borrow the Mona Lisa for show and tell. It's not happening.

But...

The initial fade is happening. A few of the hot local females just left, and the DJ's juice is spent. I've got an idea.

I'm scared out of my mind to ask, but I really like her.

"Raúl. Tengo un idea por entretenimiento." I give it all I've got. That I'm trying to impress this girl and that I think I can keep people in the bar for a bit longer. He snickers and laughs. Either at the projected profits or plain happiness that I'm not gay.

"OK. Pero tranquilo. Muy tranquilo." Keep it mellow, white boy.

I walk over to a crowd of raging gringos. No surprise, it's not happening enough here, and they're talking about heading over to Mondo Taitu, because so and so is spinning.

"Hey, guys. Could you do me a favor? My girl's necklace dropped in the water. It's a family heirloom—so I'm going to try to dive in and get it. Would you mind seeing if you can spot it?"

Who doesn't love a treasure hunt? They tell EVERYONE in the bar, and The Wreck is instantly abuzz with onlookers, all thinking that they see it. I nod to Raúl. He smartly takes over the bar and can't sell drinks fast enough. I ask the DJ to play the *Mission Impossible* theme song.

I grab my goggles and walk over to Andrea. The desire to show competence and heroism peaks during courtship.

"You are NOT…"

"I am. Point to where you think it is."

PJ reaches down and moves the nearest floodlight.

Mistake.

Raúl sees this and looks like he's going to slash the tires of a wheelchair. But the drinking revelry has returned, and cash is flowing. Andrea looks in the water, forlorn.

"It's down there somewhere…"

"MATE! It's gotta glimma! I think I can see it!" PJ points. I turn to Andrea.

"Watch my stuff, OK?"

"Of course! Be careful!" I pop off my shirt and shorts. My Speedo is already intact. Even the party bros are into it. The DJ one-ups me, with the theme song to *007*.

I slide into the water and take a deep breath.

I'm glad my goggles are new and not smudged, because the lit-up Wreck looks insane. I dive down and find her necklace almost instantly. I stealthily tuck it into my Speedo and swim a little further. It's incredible down here. Barnacles lean off of the bow, and starfish are absolutely everywhere. I milk it for all it's worth. I can vaguely hear shouting from above. It's been a solid minute. I surface. Even though there's a ladder a few feet away, PJ yanks me up onto the landing with his muscles, because he can.

Everyone can see my empty hands, and the crowd sighs in disappointment. Andrea looks sad but appreciative. I step back, soaking wet, create some room for dramatic effect and reach into my Speedo.

Anticipation.

Is he gonna pull out his dick?

"Did you drop something?"

I hand her the necklace. Bam. The crowd roars. The DJ cranks up the volume. PJ pick-up-hugs me, drenching his shirt.

"I TOLD YOU MY MATE WAS A LEGEND!"

Andrea hugs me. And hugs me. And hugs me. I pull back. She grabs my face and kisses my forehead ten times.

"Thank you thank you thank you…"

"My pleasure. Let me grab a towel. But be here when I get back, OK?" She hands me my clothes. They're are all wet and wrinkled from our hugfest.

"I'll be right here! Nice Speedo, Aquaman!" I make a mental note to leave normal trunks here. Always.

I change in the dry storage. You know, next to the huge gun. The moment I pop out to the bar, it's full celebrity status. Jäger shots, etc.

The DJ is cranking through his repertoire of suspense and crime-solving beats. He remixes the *Inspector Gadget* theme song.

Solid.

Raúl is doing his favorite thing—counting money. Andrea's posse is being coveted by a couple of predatory Bocas expats. They make PJ look like a kindergarten teacher. Damn, they are tan. Andrea walks up.

"Thank you, again. So much. This necklace means the world to me."

"Oh, no worries. It was fun. I've always wanted to dive down there."

"This place is pretty damn cool! Hey, PJ invited us over to your house for a drink, but we have to take a boat there?"

"Yeah, we live on Carenero, not far from where you were at Aqua. It's a quick trip. But I've gotta be honest, it's tough to get a boat-taxi back here late at night. One of us can probably take you in the dingy, but…"

"We are game to hang out!" She reaches up and whispers in my ear, "But I'm not having sex with you, OK?"

Isn't it the best when your new crush says, *I'm totally down to hang out!* Aka—I packed a toothbrush.

"Understood. Who says I'd have sex with you? No, seriously, come. It'll be fun to hang out. And maybe make out? You should go with PJ because I need to close up, and it takes a while."

"Perfect." She lands a bomb kiss on my lips. Whoa. She stays in for the full mack and massages my arms while she's at it. Damn, she is strong. My personal cupid, PJ, rolls up. His buzz has faded, and his eyes tell me he wants it back.

"Georgie, there're four of us, we'll take a boat-taxi, ay? Keep the Minnow for yah'self."

•

Closing down takes ages. I'm glad I don't have to swim home. I pull up at our dock and tie up the S.S. Minnow. Every single light in our house is on. It's 2:30am.

"GEORGIE!"

Rails of cocaine line one of our breakfast plates. Andrea's friends giggle. Wiglaf stands guard in the corner—not impressed.

"Where is Tsvika?"

"Gone for a couple of days, mate! Interest you in nibble?" He motions to the coke.

"Let me go drop my stuff." Andrea walks up, hands all over me.

"HI! Welcome home!"

"Hey there. I'm just gonna swap my clothes out real quick." She gives me an aggressive kiss. This whole scene is not what I'd expected. But somehow, I'm not surprised.

I do a quick rinse in the shower and change clothes. I can hear them upstairs. Please god, don't let Tsvika come home early.

I can't help myself—I check my computer.

From: Shawna B.

To: Georgeous

Subject: Dissertation Schmissertation

Hey!

Where did you go? I guess if we don't talk or email for months, I can't expect you to entertain me every day, as I sit here, loathing this paper. Who picks Modern influences of Vivienne Westwood for their dissertation???

Anyway, I hope you're well.

XX

Shawna

PS Have you tried using iMessage? I know you shut your phone off, but it still might work, if you want to chat. I try to reserve email for school and my grandparents :)

Why did I read this? I remind myself: she cheated on me. I turn toward the door.

Toward Andrea.

Let's go see what the kiddies are up to.

But I can't shake her. Shawna. Who is cool enough to choose the interplay between fashion and modern art, via Vivienne Westwood, to write a doctoral thesis on?

Fuck her.

My mom is a huge Crosby, Stills & Nash fan. She used to play their cassettes in our old Pontiac, especially: *Love the One You're With*.

Indeed.

•

PJ is pouring shots of Abuelo and telling stories about his travels. Abuelo is the local rum. It's so cheap that it always seems like a good idea—until the next day. Everyone is interrupting each other—all coked out. Andrea pulls me aside, all hands again.

"Hey, I'm sorry!"

"For what?"

"The coke. PJ said you might not be very happy about it."

"No, I'm cool. I've only done it a few times. But Tsvika? If he comes home? He will be livid."

Part of me likes spiting Tsvika, by disrespecting his house. Dark secret keeping weirdo.

"No, no. Me, too! I've done it like three times! But some guy at our hostel was leaving and just GAVE IT TO US. And this seemed like a super-safe place to play, you know?" She is very sincere. And very lit up. I look over at the bag of coke. It's a big bag; it's gonna be a big night.

"Look. It's cool. It's true—I am super careful about what I do here.

It's really easy to get people talking or get on the wrong side of folks. But I agree, this is the perfect environment and the perfect night. Did you save me some?"

Since when did I become so easy-going?

"YES!"

I light up a line. WOW. All of the fatigue from the day is gone.

Hours fly by. As does the coke.

As a rule, I am against proliferating the drug vibe in Bocas. On the cocaine northbound highway, Panama is the bridge between harvest in Colombia and consumption in Costa Rica and abroad. Panama takes a small toll—a little cash to feed the family and a few bumps to spice up Saturday nights.

But Andrea is right. This is the ideal environment to experiment with recreational pharmaceuticals. We separate into two camps: Andrea and I on one side, and PJ, Riley and Amy(?) on the other. But a PJ-threesome is on the table.

We swim and make drinks and ride the rails all night. I can't keep my hands off of Andrea, but no one seems to care. We finish the entire bag of coke. Insanity.

Around 6am, PJ kicks in with the coke beachcomber story. I've heard it a million times, so I know it's time for bed.

"Mate! What're they called? The sand fishermen?" Wiglaf watches his antics. It's unclear whether Wiglaf helps settle my paranoia or increases it.

"Pescaderos de la tierra."

"Right! So these guys! They get up at the crack EVERY day! They walk the shore, ay? And check for bags of leftovah drugs! In case something dropped from a boat! Looking to win the lottery!" It's true. I see them when I wake up early, looking to score a misplaced kilo that floated ashore. The proceeds would probably replace the roof on their house. It's terrible. And smart.

I turn to Andrea.

"I'm done. Do you wanna come to bed with me?"

"Dibs on inside spoon?"

"Of course." PJ grabs the bottle of Abuelo, again, and I know they're fucked until past sunrise. We get to my room, and I've hit the wall.

"Do you want a t-shirt or something?"

"I'm good, but I'm keeping my underwear on. OK?"

"Totally fine. Plus the coke, it makes boys kinda…"

"Soft?"

"Yeah. How'd you know? I thought you'd only done it a few times?"

"Three times before! That's it! But girls talk…"

"Of course they do."

I fall into bed. She pulls all of her clothes off, with the exception of the skimpiest G-string I've ever seen. Her quads are to die for. We make out forever.

The sun peaks in. I feel a surge of blood in my man-parts, but she's gone—passed out. My eyelids get heavy, and I follow shortly.

•

I wake at noon. Andrea is still out. She's thrown the covers off, allowing me to sneak a few glances at her body.

It's time to get up. The kitchen is destroyed. PJ is unconscious in the corner chair of our living room. Checking on the girls, I see them cuddled together on PJ's bed. I need to re-ask Andrea their names. I lick my dry lips—chapped from the coke and making out with Andrea. I pound straight from a half gallon of bottled water, and PJ doesn't even stir.

Time to get wet.

The ocean feels incredible. But I'm so shattered; the thought of any legit workout is not happening. Even a shower sounds exhausting. Walking out of the water, I pray Marco doesn't come by.

Need…bed.

The sensation of crawling back in bed with Andrea is heavenly. She purrs a little at my touch, turns around and kisses me.

"I'm so tired."

"Me too. And I'm never doing coke again."

"You're sooo salty! Did you go in the water?"

"Yeah, but I was too tired to shower. Sorry."

"No, it tastes good."

Three more minutes and I hook my finger around the waistband of her panties. She lets me slide them off, without hesitation, even tilting her hips to help.

So hot.

I need to go get a condom from PJ, but it seems too far away right now. She's so wet. She pulls me into her.

"Ahhh."

"Ohhh…"

"Uhm, we should use a…ahhh." But she doesn't stop.

"I know. I don't have a condoooohhm. But I had a blood test three months ago, and I haven't had…ahhh."

"OK. OK. I…I trust you. You don't seem reckless. Oh my god, you feel so good."

I grab her face and kiss her. Everywhere. Her body is an amusement park.

I start planning our kids' names. John Grady Cole from *All the Pretty Horses* has always been a favorite.

For one second, I think about how I told this to Shawna. That I liked the name Cole.

She whips around and gets on top of me. She rides me with such voracity, it almost hurts. She rips her nails into my chest, and I can feel the clenching.

She comes.

Dropping on top of me, listless, she tries to keep moving, but she's too tired.

"Can you go again?"

"No, you go. I'm…I'm."

"You can't?"

"No, I can, just…"

"I wanna taste you."

5

How hard do you party?

    a)   You know people that have done drugs!

    b)   You ask your cokehead friends not to use the ceramic plates to cut up rails,
        but the Pyrex ones are fine.

    c)   You can buy a bag of anything you want, from a guy who knows you by
        name, drives a limo, will chit chat with you during the transaction and offer
        you a one-way ride anywhere within three miles. Convenience charge
        notwithstanding.

Andrea agreed to going on a real date, and I'm wearing the nicest thing I own—my best swim trunks and a short-sleeved shirt with a collar. While waiting, I have two drinks at the Ultimo Refugio to loosen up. Refugio has a small bar plus half a dozen tables, tucked away in a little nook. It's the perfect date spot. I check my watch and wish that I had picked her up on foot. It's only been five hours since she left our house, but it feels like a year ago.

"Hi!"

"Hey!" We kiss, but it's weird. She sits, looking awesome and dressy for Bocas. It's awkward, like a blind date.

"I can see you're already drinking."

"I'm a little nervous."

"I'm a little nervous, too. I've never really had a one night stand and then a date after."

"That was not a one night stand. It was more like five dates, back to back."

"I totally agree!"

"OK. Good. Thank you. That makes me feel a lot better."

"Me, too."

"Hey, do you want a drink? Beer or?"

"Something stronger. What's that?"

"Vodka. Ice. Lime. No mixer. Big boy drink."

"Big boy! OK! I'll take the same, but with a little soda?"

I stand up and take her hand.

"Come with me for a sec?"

"Okaaay?" On the way out, I ask the bartendress for her drink.

Spanish is pointless because Refugio has the most attractive hand-picked gringa waitstaff in town. All English speaking. She could be serving drinks in Santa Monica.

I tug Andrea's hand, and we walk out front. Kids play nearby on the makeshift playground. Drug dealing teens prospect us.

"Hey."

"Hey?"

I rest my hands on her waist, pulling her in.

"Last night was madness. But I do really like you, and I wanna hang out as much as we can while you're here. OK?" She smiles and nestles into me.

"Yeah. That would be nice." We kiss for a minute.

Chemistry restored.

"Wanna eat something? The food is amazing here."

"Yes!" She pecks me on the cheek. We walk in, hand in hand. We order a few shrimp appetizers and gaze out on the water. Then it comes. The rumble in the jungle. I excuse myself, holding my stomach.

You know any dude taking a number 2 in a bathroom stall at a gringo bar, a concert or a dive bar is either a) seriously ill, b) doing coke or c) suffering from the coke shits. John Mayer had it right in his YouTube video; the coke shits are the worst. And this is one of those places with limited sanitation—aka no toilet paper allowed in the toilet.

Ugh.

I return to our table, embarrassed.

"Everything OK?"

"The coke. It's, uh…"

"Oh my god, I know! Riley and Aurora were sick all day! Are you OK? Do you wanna go?"

Got it: Aurora, not Amy.

"No. I'm good. You're sweet. I'm fine. Can we change the subject? I could tell you a racy story about how I learned about sex in grade school? Real quick, before the appetizers come?"

"Yes! Let's hear it!"

"So, when I was a kid, taking the bus to school, one of the older kids had an uncle that would field our 'coming of age' questions."

"That's frightening."

"It was probably seventh grade? And we asked him on some Friday, who sex felt better for—the boy or the girl? We all waited eagerly for Monday morning."

"And?"

"We snuck off to the side of the bus stop, and he spilled it. I don't remember exactly, but it was something like, 'When you scratch your ear, what feels better? Your finger or your ear?'"

"Brilliant. And so true."

"Why don't you tell me about how, if I come to Portland, you will be my personal barista?"

"HA! I'll have my staff make you whatever you like. I don't make coffee drinks myself."

"Oooh. Bossy."

We eat. And walk. And take the boat back. And fuck. She comes like a superstar. I faintly hear Wiglaf grumble.

She wants me to come, too—so badly. I'm trying hard to dig her, but somehow I find myself involuntarily fantasizing about Shawna, just so I can finish.

Terrible.

But she'll be crushed if she can't get me off on the third try. So the Shawna bit feels like the lesser of the two evils.

And, finally, it works.

And she's ecstatic.

And I feel awful.

"Hey, do you wanna take an ATV out to Playa Bluff tomorrow?"

"YES!"

She showers me with kisses, and I feel less bad. But only slightly.

•

I need to write Shawna back, even though I don't really owe her anything. We tried to stay amicably in touch after her initial trip out here, but the third breakup tends to stick. I thought I was a bigger man, but I never totally recovered from her infidelity. I never knew—and she clearly never knew—that I was so possessive. Our emails petered out a few weeks after she left.

I'm not stupid. Shawna is gorgeous. Surely she found someone to help her solidify our break-up, just as I am trying to do with Andrea.

Andrea's newness, hmmm.

Somehow she kills the day-to-day loneliness, yet makes me miss Shawna more. There's nothing more difficult than forcing yourself to be satisfied.

Fucking Shawna. She must suspect that the abrupt end of our sexy emails means that I've met someone. I do some triage of my feelings and write her.

From: Georgeous

To: Shawna B.

Subject: missing in action

hey. thanks for your note, and sorry i've been off the grid. i think your thesis (appropriate pseudonym for dissertation?) sounds awesome. i thought you might choose jean paul gaultier, but vivienne is way more punk rock. it says fuck you to your phd of fine arts cohorts. so stick with it. at least you got into grad school, unlike one of us ;)

a lot of crazy stuff has happened. remember when you went bananas on that guy in ventura (yet another romantic dinner i planned that was thwarted), on his second amendment right to bear arms? well, let's just say that constitutional right is thriving here in bocas.

with love, from the ghetto paradise.

george

An email from TR has been sitting in my inbox for a day and a half.

From: Rogers, Timothy

To: Georgeous

Subject: RE: On time on budget

George—

Happy to be your advocate anytime. You have a decent amount of talent and a surplus of reliability. The latter being the most critical in this business. Hopefully, we'll always have a spot for you.

Thanks again for turning that around so quickly. And the only person we have to check your grammar is you. I'm sure whatever changes you made are fine.

Cheers,

TR

PS Please don't respond to this, but if you really do know a cocaine-

dealing limo driver, about half of Manhattan would love to have
his/her phone number.

It's impossible that Shawna has not read my email. It's daytime.
She's in front of her computer all day long, cranking out her
dissertation. She'd kill for any distraction. But this is the game we play.
You make me wait; I make you wait.

PJ is chilling in the kitchen, drinking coffee I made hours ago. His
shirt today is yet another one of my favorites: *You say tomato, I say*
tomaGMO. Appropriate, as pulling breakfast from our empty pantry will
require some creativity.

"Hey, where has the Tsviks been?"

I have a few of questions for him.

"He's been around, ay! It's just that you're all shacked up now, with
yah new bird!"

"Fair. I wouldn't say I miss him. It's just weird how much he
comes and goes."

And how he finds certain people photogenic.

"The Tsviks and I are headin' over to The Bluffs today. Mind if we
take the skiff?"

"Really? You two, together? That's cute. We'll pass right by.
Andrea and I are going to rent an ATV."

"Aw mate! You've really fallen, ay? Taking Jane back to the
jungle?"

"Um, fuck off?"

"Easy, mate. She's a good one. Why dontcha meet us there? We're looking at a bit of property. Come give us a look? Maybe meet for a bottle of piss at Bom Bom? From town, it'll take you guys about an hour?"

"You're looking to put down roots here? And you're taking our resident real estate expert? That is absurd and fantastic. Have we confirmed that Tsvika is actually in the real estate business?"

Maybe the ambient light at Bluff makes it easier to launch a reconnaissance satellite?

"Who cares, mate? The guy is connected! I told him roughly where it was, on the jungle side of Bluff, and he pulled up the plot on his computah!"

"Aerial photos from a drone?"

"Ay?"

"Never mind. Sounds great."

•

The quad is gassed up and ready to go. Andrea walks up. I hand her a helmet. The Flying Pirate offers a self-guided tour along the beach. It's structured, with signs along the way, but you still feel outdoorsy, as you're on your own and have to navigate the sandy roads. It's thrilling to plow through the mud and rev the motor. Riding quads, doing cocaine in a safe place...we all want to dip our toes into the deep end of the pool. Then we quickly lean back from the edge, so we don't fall in.

Andrea does look cute with her helmet on.

"Ready?"

"Let's go, Fonzie!"

I haven't driven a car in almost a year. Even driving the ATV through town feels unreal. It's scary, too, with the pickup truck cabbies flying by.

If someone hits us, we're fucked.

Against my advice, Andrea is wearing flip-flops. My canvas sneakers are already soaked in sweat, but wearing flip-flops to stomp on the gearshift is not an option. We hit the dirt road, and she tightens her grip around my waist.

"Weee!"

At Paki Point, we pull over to let an oncoming jitney pass. We sit for a while, letting the quad idle, checking out the backpackers lazing in hammocks.

"Can we go there?"

"For sure. Maybe tomorrow? We can take a cab and hang out all day. Your friends can come, too."

"Perfect!" We roll on and traverse a river with about an inch of water in it.

"This is so fun!"

I feel like Vasco de Gama.

Wait—where's that sign that tells us which way to turn?

We pull up at Bar Bom Bom. It's a picturesque beachfront bamboo shack, with only outdoor seating. PJ and Tsvika are being served by another gringa. They all have the same story, "I came here for a week, and then I stayed another week, and then I ran out of money." I call them Brokeass del Tourists. They get stuck here, handing out beers for $1.50/hour plus tips, until their parents finally cave and send them a plane ticket. This one will arrive back in the suburbs, with twenty new words of Spanish, three bracelets (they were handmade!) and four sarongs that she'll never wear again. I hate how much it sounds like me.

"Well, well, well. We're getting the band back together."

"Georgie! Hello, dollface! How was the trip?"

"Oh my god! I could do this EVERY DAY!"

"Yeah, it's pretty dope. You feel like you're pioneering the jungle, until you see the little Flying Pirate arrow at every crossroad. ATVs with training-wheels. What's up Tsviks? Nice to see you out and about."

Tsvika is not one for subtle sarcasm.

"PJ, he makes me come. To look at the place for the school."

"School?"

"Surf school, mate! There's a little bit of land up the way, build a couple of huts, nice and clean. Rent 'em. Give surf lessons. Take ressies over the intahnet…"

"Cool!" Andrea's optimism is bottomless.

"Dude. I feel like I don't even know you any more. Since when did you get so…ambitious? You would really live here? Forever?"

"And there's a jungle full of kids you can teach to swim, partnah!"

"Partner? Are you fucking kidding?" He looks a little hurt, so I pump the brakes. "OK, let's go check it out. I want to show Andrea the beach at Mimbi Timbi anyway, and it's gotta be on the way, right?"

"The land is just up the road!"

This isn't the best time, but I've gotta do it.

"Hey, can you guys grab another drink? I want Tsviks to take a look at my clutch on the quad."

"Fa shore, mate! I'll keep an eye on yah bird!"

Andrea is enchanted by the crashing waves. PJ orders. They aren't remotely suspicious. But still, my heart is racing.

We get a few feet from the ATV.

"The clutch? Is sticking? These ones…small motor…"

"Shut the fuck up."

"George?"

"Why do you have enough maps to run the National Geographic Society, a gun and pictures of me and Raúl?"

He takes a breath. Then another.

"George. We talk later. Not now." He glances over his shoulder at PJ. "At home."

"Fine, you fucking creeper. But you need to know two things right now—I'd better not be some sort of fucking cover for you. And I have info on Raúl."

"At home."

"Trust me. You want this information. Or do you guys call it 'intel'?"

I glare at him for a long second.

"Fuck it. Let's go." I start walking back and then whisper over my shoulder, "And no, I'm not gonna tell PJ."

PJ is talking about his family's move from Melbourne to Sydney, when he was fourteen, and how many fights he and his brother got into, overreacting to their sister's suitors. His sister is my age—three years older. That means that PJ, at fourteen, was stepping to seventeen and eighteen year olds—fearless, even as an adolescent. It's charming that the biggest philanderer on earth is such a family man.

"Yeah, I was a scrappy little grom, ay?"

Andrea is eating up every word. Their fun-loving normalcy calms me.

Tsviks and I have been gone eight minutes, and PJ has already put two beers down. They pay their tab to the future suburban housewife, and we roll out. I'm a dick. She's probably an attorney back home.

PJ's got a point. It is beautiful up here. No trash. And it's still close enough to town that you could import a refrigerator from the mainland on a ferry. It's much more turnkey than trying to pull this off by our house, where everything has to come by a small boat.

I'm getting sucked in. Andrea grabs my hand like we've been dating for years. I love the attention, but I'm secretly glad that no one can see us.

"It's so gorgeous up here! Do you think we might see a sloth?"

"Maybe. Keep your eyes out. Just be careful of the howler monkeys. The last time I was hiking here, I set my bag down, pulled out a snack and one of those fuckers swooped down and snagged my Pure Protein bar. It was the last of the Trader Joe's treats I'd brought over on the plane. Why would a monkey want twenty grams of protein? Little bastard."

"Seriously?"

"Swear."

Tsvika is eavesdropping, as always.

"You like hike? Next time, bring Wiglaf. Wiglaf love monkey."

Jesus. Is he trying to impress Andrea?

Nope.

Just continuing to be a weirdo, as always.

"It's right up there on the right! If we put the bungalows on stilts, they'd have a bit of an ocean view!" PJ's enthusiasm is contagious. Tsvika gives it a thorough review. Good spot for a gun range?

We walk the property. It looks legit. It even has PVC pipe laid out, for the water lines.

"How much?"

"$40K."

"Whoa. Just for the land? This is what, a quarter acre?"

"Give it to us in hectares, mate?"

"Um, about a tenth?" I double-check my calculation by looking at Andrea. She shrugs. I tease. "Oh, right. You're all about promoting the metric system."

We walk back down the hill. I can't help but look back at it, daydreaming. The boys head down to grab the S.S. Minnow, which is tied up in a neighboring bay. PJ makes one more plug.

"Give us a think on it, mate?"

"I will. I promise. See you guys back at the ranch."

Andrea and I hit up the Playa Bluff Lodge, sip drinks and look at the amazing view.

Heading back to return the quad is bittersweet. I don't want this day to end.

"So, shall I drop you off for some quality time with your friends, or do you wanna come home with me?"

"What does George want me to do?"

"Of course I want you to come with me, but I don't want to hold you hostage. Your girls must want to hang with you, right?"

"Aren't they coming tomorrow to the Pocky Place?"

"Paki Point. Of course. I was thinking the same thing. Plus we can all share a cab. It's cheaper. Maybe PJ will come, too. He's one of the only people with the balls to surf there."

"Awesome! OK! Let's go to your house!"

We retrieve our passports, grab a boat-taxi and head back.

It's dusk. Good thing I have my waterproof flashlight handy.

"WOOOGHF."

"That dog is terrifying."

"I know. But I like having him around." I scratch Wiglaf's ears. "It's a bit intense for a welcome home, but there is not a chance that we will ever get robbed. He's the most territorial dog I've ever seen. If he doesn't know you, and you tossle Tsvika's hair—I mean, who wouldn't want to, right?—Wiglaf will rip your face off."

"Jesus."

"You said it, man. Nobody fucks with the Jesus."

"Is that a movie quote?

"Never mind."

Little Marco's head pops into view, at the sliding glass door.

"Marquito! Qué paso?" He shrugs but walks toward us. "Traje la linterna." I hand him my flashlight. "Quieres nadar conmigo?" He hesitates, even though I know he came to swim. Andrea must be making him shy.

"Sí, si quieres." He palms my coveted waterproof flashlight, with clipping carabiner. When I rule the world, everything will illuminate, be magnetic, waterproof, reversible, float and have a clip. I'm still seeking a lightweight jacket that meets these requirements.

"What's happening? The flashlight?"

"It's a little game we play called Fetchlight. Come on, let's go change."

"Marquito, esperas un minuto, OK?"

"OK." He switches the flashlight on and off. Then, he watches us walk back into the house, skeptically. He knows girls make boys disappear, but he's satisfied with a valuable toy as collateral. In my room, we start taking our clothes off. I stop to admire her, with just my shirt on. She stares at me changing, unselfconsciously.

"Really? You're Donald Duckin' it?"

"Huh?"

"Shirt on, naked below, you look like Donald Duck."

"Wow. True. Is that really a thing?"

"For sure."

"I like it." I walk around the room, trying to own it. But I feel ridiculous and take my shirt off.

She's so fun. I can't figure out why my attraction to her lacks something. On paper, she's perfect for me.

"Mind if I shower?"

"Of course not."

"Wanna come?"

"I can't believe I'm saying no, but I haven't seen Marco in a couple of days. If I don't get some water time with him, he'll probably try to build a pipe bomb."

"Oh, right. Go. I'll be up in a minute."

I throw on a pair of boardshorts, grab two pairs of goggles and head out to meet Marquito. He's surprised that I'm back so soon.

That makes two of us.

True to form, the flashlight has kept him entertained.

I hand Marquito the goggles.

"Listo?"

"Sí."

The remaining sunlight is fading fast. Perfect timing. I take the flashlight back and chuck it with all I've got. I'm no Peyton Manning, but it's pretty deep in the bay for an eight-year-old. He goes after it like a golden retriever. After a few throws, Andrea comes out, looking both clean and dirty.

"What a cool game! It's so simple! Look at the light reflecting off the bottom when he swims! So beautiful!" I kiss her.

So beautiful.

"Yeah, this is how I'll make my millions, entertaining children with cheap tricks. Do you wanna toss it?"

"Sure!"

Marco hands it over.

I can tell by Marco's face that he's thinking: *chicks can't throw.* But he's wrong. Her lean climber's arm cocks back, and she launches it. Little Marco turns back and looks at her.

Respect.

He swims for it and returns. Andrea is elated.

"One more time?"

"He looks a little beat. Lemme see."

"Marquito, quieres nadar conmigo?" He finishes catching his breath.

"Sí, sí."

"I'm gonna cruise in with him for a bit. Cool?"

"Okaaay!" I pick up my goggles, and we walk in. Within seconds, he jumps on my back. Jortuga in effect. Our little bay can be eerie at night, but the bottom is mostly sand. I can drag us along with my feet. I feel him fidget for air, and we head up.

"You guys disappeared! What's that game called?"

"Jortuga. Long story."

"Marquito…a casa." Marco, it's time for you to go home.

"Sí. Es tarde." He heads down the path, shoulders slumped. He turns back and mumbles, "Gracias." He's so sweet when he's tired.

"He's going to walk home by himself? He's soaking wet!"

"He's fine. Trust me. He's the safest kid on this island."

●

"I need to go pay Tsvika my rent. Can you entertain yourself for a few minutes?"

"Of course. Is there any chance you have lotion?"

"Yeah, there's some after-sun stuff and a tube of aloe in my bathroom."

"Perfect."

I head down to Tsvika's room.

With my head in the doorway, he can see it in my eyes.

"What is it? Mossad?"

Silence.

"I was fucking joking, but now I'm not so sure. What's your deal, Tsvika?"

"Why you go to Colombia?"

"To teach swimming, you dick."

"Just the swimming? With Raúl?"

"Tsvika, I went for the ride. OK? I didn't know he was going to be transporting a fucking machine gun."

Now I have his attention.

"Gun? You have seen?"

6

When do you tell your girl that you love her?

 a) Immediately before you have sex for the first time.

 b) The day you propose.

 c) After she waits six months for it, and then she finally baits you with,
   "You know I love you, right?"

 d) The moment you feel it.

PJ's board juts off the front of the Minnow. It looks like something we're going to drop off at the dump. All of the fins are mismatched, it's yellow from age and has enough ding fixes to make it look like an old man with liver spots. His shorts continue the theme—ripped and faded. I've re-sewn his top button three times.

But once he's in the water?

He will dominate.

We're lucky we can always park the boat at The Wreck. Deliveries arrive constantly. Multiple sets of eyes are everywhere. Our humble little Zodiac is safe. Life is convenient when you are complicit in drug sales and felony weapons trafficking.

PJ, Andrea and I tie up. We're not alone. Four hard-looking dudes are unloading cargo that is absolutely not bar supplies. Coke? Machine guns? Probably both. Raúl watches us watch them.

"Raúl, todo bien?" All good?

"Claro. Adonde vas?" What are you up to, gringo?

"Punta Paki. Con las chicas. Quieres vengar? Por un cervecito?" I invite him to come for a beer.

"No, gracias. Punta Paki, las mujeres se encantan, no?" He's right. The ladies love Paki Point. It's the postcard of what you should be doing in the Caribbean.

Absolutely nothing.

And they serve drinks.

The offer for him to come with us is a bit shallow, but I'd love to sit with him in a neutral place sometime. Today? It's not happening. This is another one of those fake conversations, where every ten times we talk, he acts like he gives a shit. I do the exact same thing back.

"Clarisimo. Todo bien con El Barco?" I look around the bar and at The Wreck.

"Sí, sí."

Shady motherfucker.

At least there's free parking.

We pick up Andrea's crew on foot, before getting a cab. They are beach-dressed to the nines. They've got bags of gear we don't need, waiting by the door.

"You guys expecting Armageddon, ay?"

"PJ! We need that stuff!" PJ has his board, no shirt and $34. I like their banter. It says, "We partied together, did a bag of coke and almost fucked. Now it's totally cool to hang at the beach." Riley is not oblivious to his body, though. Here we go again. Andrea scans the streets.

"We should probably get one of those four door trucks, huh? How do you say truck in Spanish?"

"Formally, I think it's camioneta. But everyone here says troca."

"Just like truck! That's easy!"

"Yeah, there are so many cognates in Spanish. Like how auto and auto are the same. But you have to be careful when you guess, because there are some landmines."

"Like?"

"Like how you'd think embarazada would mean embarrassed, right? But it means pregnant."

"Oh god."

"Or esposa? It means spouse. But esposas, plural, means handcuffs. That's my favorite."

"That is terrible."

We find a taxi, and everyone looks at me to negotiate.

Although they usually try to squeeze a few more dollars out of the gringos, the Bocas cabbies are unbelievably patient. We take forever getting situated into the cab, and he doesn't bat an eye. Five people plus our gear—it looks like we're cramming into a clown car. I'm tallest and have to sit in front. Aurora (another yuppie kid's name) does NOT want her beach bag in the truck bed. I'm trying to remember if I ever called her Amy to her face. PJ has already tucked their bags under his board. He's tying it all down with a thin piece of twine that was probably thrown into the bed of the truck as trash.

"Our stuff is gonna fly out!"

"Ahhh, babe! What are we gonna hit? Forty k's per hour tops, ay? We're good. Giddy up!"

We make four stops along the way. Riley is on PJ's lap. There's no room for a local to jump in with us, as would normally happen. At each bodega, our driver exchanges an empty pack of cigarettes with someone for…another empty pack of cigarettes. He's a drug mule. Fortunately, he's driving at a safe speed. As far as I'm concerned, his entrepreneurial spirit is his own business.

Halfway there, he pulls over and drops two cigarette packs into a black plastic bag that's sitting amongst other garbage. His drug mailbox. You'd think he'd be worried that we'd steal it, or that other locals might, but none of us are that stupid. Although PJ takes note. Madman.

Paki Point delivers. Sun. Hammocks. Loungey chairs. The place makes you thirsty for beers and chill time. Riley and Aurora are thrilled.

"This place is ahhhmazing!"

"I told you guys! Isn't it incredible?"

The surf looks perfect. The waves are big, breaking on the outside reef. PJ unloads all the gear like a Sherpa. I handle the finances with the cabbie. Maybe the surf school could work? He grabs his board and unceremoniously shouts over his shoulder.

"Catch you kiddies in a bit."

Ten seconds later, he's in the water. The break at Paki Point is surrounded by rocks. Novice gringo surfers cautiously put on booties, fearful of the reef. PJ walks out across it, like he's parting the Red Sea. The locals own this spot, but they give PJ the bro nod.

"Beers?"

"Yes!"

We try to pick a spot, but the girls want sun, and Andrea and I want shade. We separate. A few male German backpackers wait patiently for each of the them to undress.

Holy rack, Riley. You've been hiding that this whole time? But Andrea's stomach tops all. I wanna build a house on top of it and live there.

PJ carves the shit out of a right-hander. The girls wave and take photos.

"Wow. He's really good!"

"That guy has more natural physical talent than anyone I've ever met. He's the hardest man alive. It's not fair. But it couldn't happen to a nicer guy."

"You really love him, don't you?"

"I do."

"You should have heard him the night we met at The Wreck Deck. Georgie this and Georgie that. He teaches the kids! He's so smaaart."

"Yeah, he's my PR guy."

"So, the surf school is a go? You're thinking about it?" Is she fishing for info about our future? Our beers come. Ice cold. Delicious.

"To be honest, I thought it was a pipe dream. But now? It could be possible. I have a little cash. Not that much, but I could probably get ahold of half."

"Tsvika's not investing?"

"Tsvika?" I almost spit my beer out. "It hadn't even crossed my mind. But now that you say it, he would be a great angel investor. I live with him but probably only see him five percent of the time. And he knows people. Everywhere." I toast her for the insight.

Maybe the Israeli government wants to invest, too? Write it off as a paramilitary outpost?

"You should do it. It's ballsy, but it's not that much money. And you could live HERE. Incredible." The day before on the ATVs, she had been looking at The Bluffs with her climber's eyes. People do climb them. And some of The Bluffs even have climbing nuts and chalk marks.

"I might. Would you come? I never really imagined my life one hundred percent outside of the States. I was considering going home soon. I can work—at least right now—from anywhere. Even Oregon." I smile, seeing if she bites.

I'm not sure if I really want her to come back or if there's any chance that I'd go visit her. It just feels like what I should want to do. What I should say.

"Uhhh." She takes a sip of her beer and sits back. "George, I have a guy in Portland."

"A guy?"

"Yeah, sort of."

"Like a boyfriend?"

"Uhhh, yeah."

"How long have you been seeing him?"

"Off and on for three years. He's kind of an asshole, but I love him, you know?"

"I know...what? That you have a boyfriend?"

"Easy, tiger. I didn't mean to upset you. I just..."

"You just what?"

"I wanted to come on vacation. An actual vacation. Not just a trip somewhere. And you made it a vacation. You did that for me. Thank you. And you've been so sweet. But Portland? That's not a good idea."

Brutal. We sit in silence for a few minutes.

"So, I'm just stupid for really liking you?"

"No, no. You're amazing. And if circumstances were different?" She takes a long sip of her beer. "But come on, George. What did you really think? You're a bartender in the Caribbean...this must happen all the time..."

"It doesn't." I sigh. But trying to act legitimately mad feels forced. "I need to use the restroom."

When I return, we stay silent. PJ exits the water. Thank god. He rinses at the outdoor shower, soft porn for every female at the bar, and walks over. I've already ordered a beer for him. Andrea packs up.

"I'm gonna try to get a little tan with the girls." PJ throws her a big smile.

"Nice one!" She walks over to Riley and Aurora, who are giggling.

"Why the long face? Trouble in paradise?"

"She has a boyfriend back home. Three years."

"Awww. 'Course she does! They all do!" He inhales half of his beer. "She's a good girl, and you're a bit traditional, but didja really think she was the one? Mate…"

"Yeah? No. I, I don't know. I think? I just thought…"

"Thought that you could get over Shawna by shagging her? And it would all work out?"

"Yeah?"

"Girls don't come here to meet guys like you, mate. They come here to get away from guys like you. It's part of your charm, ay?"

PJ soft-punches me in the shoulder. But his eyes tell me he feels bad for delivering the tough love.

Charming fucker.

We sit and watch the waves for ages, sinking a few more beers. I look over at Andrea. She's in full tanning mode. Not a care in the world. I look for a clock, but like every bar in Bocas, there isn't one. Marketing genius.

Either ten minutes or three hours goes by. I look at the sun, and it's probably been closer to four hours. Fuck it's hot, even though there's a fan right above us.

No, no, no…I look up and grimace.

The fan isn't moving.

"Fuck." PJ can read the slightest intonations of my swearing. For such a simple guy, he's a bit Jedi.

"Naaah, you've got to be keeeding me!"

"Yep."

"The powah is off, again! It's like we're in a bloody third-world country!" I pull out my janky island cell phone and text Giovani, my go-to guy.

Pt Paki? 5 pass. $20.

He writes back instantly. I upped the ante a little, from $15 to $20, but it's worth it.

---

en cam

Phew. "En cam" is slang for, "en mi camino"—I'm on my way. The crew behind the counter finally notices.

"Aye. Sin luz." They do absolutely nothing about it.

It sucks, but just like at the print shop, I love hearing this phrase. Spanish is so simple, elegant. Sin luz = no light. Sin techo = no roof. Calling someone "homeless" wouldn't mean anything in Spanish—so what? You're without a home? That's no biggie. But to say sin techo— dude, you've got no roof? That sucks. English is unnecessarily complicated.

"Ladies. Sorry to interrupt the tanning sesh. Not sure if you've noticed, but the power is out. And it's late enough that if we don't go now, we could be stuck here or have to walk home. It's at least three miles. I already called us a cab. Be ready in five, OK?"

"Oh, jeez, OK."

When the power goes out, people go home to lock up their shit, have sex and drink the beer while it's still cold. Cabbies are people, too. You've gotta get them quick.

Wondering about whether power-outage-sex saves marriages reminds me of being in bed with Andrea. Sadness hits, but it's brief. This couldn't be a cleaner getaway. I'm not so sure I would have gone to Oregon, anyway.

I ask for our bill. We ordered two pizzas at $7.50 apiece and ten beers at $1.50 apiece. That's $30. Calculating the bill takes ten minutes.

Giovani delivers. I wish I could call him "clutch" in Spanish, but it wouldn't translate. PJ sorts out the gear, and the girls load up. It feels like the end of summer vacation. And to think I had been fantasizing about maybe spending Christmas with Andrea, all bundled up, in the States. But instead, I'll still be here. And it'll be eighty-five degrees.

Belize Navidad.

"Mil gracias, amigo."

"Nada…"

Giovani plays on the Bocas baseball team. Homeboy can hit. I've seen him. We've got stagnant break-up air in the cab, so I chat with him about their team this year. He's a quiet, humble guy. Baseball is one of the few topics he'll talk about. He will be our go-to guy if PJ's Surf School and Shag Shack takes off. A couple of twenty-dollar airport pick-ups a week would be huge for him.

No, I don't know why he has an Italian name. And no, I don't know why jean shorts look good on him. Only locals can pull off jean shorts.

Even though he is quiet, Giovani has invited me out to drink beer and watch their team with his family. I've walked by and watched a few games as an interloper. I need to take him up on it. Other locals will serve you a drink and be all smiles one night and then scowl at you, as they pass by on their beach cruiser the next day. But I guess it's the same everywhere, even at home. Here it's just more pronounced, because you always feel like you're on the outside.

Always.

The local-to-gringo relationship is like an allergy sufferer depending on Zyrtec-D. It makes you groggy, but you can't live without it.

We pull up at their crib and unload. Riley gives me a sheepish hug. Andrea must have told her.

"George, you've been fantastic. Really made our trip. I hope we can return the favor sometime. Let us know if you're ever in Oregon!"

"Nah, you guys were great. So much fun. Even spring break has to end sometime, right?"

"Not for you!"

Hugs all around. PJ sets his board on the broken sidewalk and totes their gear up. Andrea stops short, in front of me.

"We don't leave until the last flight tomorrow, if you…"

"I gotta work."

I can see her relief. I hug her and give her a kiss on the cheek.

"You know, if…"

I interrupt her, again.

"Andrea, you know where to find me. OK? Travel safe."

She stands on her tippy toes and kisses me on the lips. I can't help myself. Full-blown make out with another dude's girl.

PJ returns.

"Saddle up!"

Andrea gives me a half-smile and heads up the stairs. We head toward the Minnow. I'm already holding the flashlight. The Wreck is an even more bizarre place with the sun setting. Untying the ropes, a used diaper floats by. I hate this place for a second. For all of the love I have for this island, goddamn, it sure is fickle toward me.

Surfboard across my legs, flashlight pointed forward, PJ steps to the back, yanks the chord and starts the Minnow in one pull. Our teamwork is unstoppable, even when I'm a grumpy bastard.

"WOOOGHF." I'm actually glad to see Wiglaf. I pet his head on the way in. He accepts it, but no tail wagging—that shows weakness.

When I come out of the shower, PJ is reaching into the fridge.

"Bottle of piss?"

"Absolutely." He hands me one. "And that shirt? Genius."

He looks down at: *Career Center—We're Hiring!*

"It was the only freshie I had left!"

"I haven't seen *Mozzarella Stick Vegetarian* in a while?"

"Think one of the girls nicked it!"

"Hopefully it was a tourist and not a local. Everyone knows you by that shirt."

"All's fair in love and war, mate."

"Love, loss. The purpose of life escapes me."

A tiny gecko drops from the ceiling onto the kitchen counter. I want to tame him and train him to sleep on my chest, to eat that one mosquito that might give me dengue fever.

"Nah. The purpose of life? It's all about getting a blowie, in a piping hot showah, while eating mint chip ice cream!"

"That's the goal of life. For you, anyway. Love and loss probably oversimplify eighty years on earth. In twenty year segments, it's closer to: destroy, repair, build and decay."

"Pretty dark, mate. That's you're goal? Nah. Life? It's all about doing whatcha love and hangin' with yah mates!"

It hurts me how right he is. I show him my empty beer.

"Nice one! Welcome back from the othah side, Georgie!"

Tsvika and a random Israeli dude cruise into the kitchen. He hands PJ a printout.

"Land survey. Of the place."

"Thanks, Tsviks!"

We don't bother exchanging names with his buddy. Tsvika has an abundant rotation of introverted guests. All they do is hang out in his room. He grabs some cheese from the fridge, our only box of crackers (which I bought) and heads back down to the cave. I used to think that Tsvika and his buddies were the shy video game players, always keeping to themselves. And PJ and I were the meatheads—hanging out upstairs, crushing beers on our foreheads.

Now I know better.

Either one of these soft-spoken weirdos could kill PJ or me in one blow.

Nerdy Krav Maga motherfuckers.

I wonder if Tsvika's sleepover buddy knows that I'm sniffing out the plot.

PJ turns the papers toward me. Tsvika included some recent land sale data, too.

Smart.

PJ's subtlety about roping me into his Surf & Shag Shack fantasy is not so subtle. I do my best impression of his voice.

"Doin' whatcha love and hangin' with yah mates?"

"Cheers, partnah!"

•

I suppress the subterfuge that I'm intertwined in and embrace island-time.

It works.

The days fly by. I find myself checking the date on my computer, so that I don't miss shifts at The Wreck.

Shawna surfaces.

From: Shawna B.

To: Georgeous

Subject: YAAAY!

I'm done! I defended yesterday and passed! I am Dr. Shawna! I've already gotten fifteen calls from major universities looking for a Fine Arts Professor! Just kidding. I have zero job prospects, but my advisor told me I could stay on as a post-doc. It's only $60k a year, but that's twice what I make now. Better than nothing, right?

Anyway, you probably don't care. But I had to tell you.

I have 3 weeks off and nowhere to go! God, reading a fashion
magazine and watching TV sounds amazing.

XX

Shawna

PS No attempt at iMessage? Must be your new Panamanian girlfriend
keeping tabs on you ;)

It's nice to hear her voice. It pulls me out of my funk. Why am I so
weak for her?

From: Georgeous

To: Shawna B.

Subject: that is so fucking AWESOME!

oh, shawna, that is great. so, so great. i feel like a weird old grandpa
saying this, but i'm proud of you. long haul, eh?
i have to run. the boat needs oil, and we've got a few errands while
we're out. but i will try imessage. i heard last week at the bar that it
works, even on a suspended stateside phone number. how would we
survive without the icloud? i'll pause being a luddite, as your graduation
present. probably tomorrow.
you are always welcome to come here and read elle magazines. sorry,
no tv ;)

g

Our boat is a two-stroker, which means you have to mix the oil and the gas together. It's messy, and half of it ends up in the water. My next non-profit is going to be becoming a small engine mechanic and touring all of Latin America tuning engines. The gasoline savings and water quality improvements would be massive.

PJ is on fire. He's full throttle on this Playa Bluff thing. He's even teeing up a swim clinic for me—focusing on the kids that live near The Bluffs. He made a new flyer and already had it printed (what?). He left the date blank this time. That way, we can Sharpie it in right before—in case of any snafus or the dreaded *sin luz*.

Genius.

He's been beavering away in his room, mocking up the website. We'd kicked around a few names, but my worst one he loves, so we're going with it. He spent most of his youth just outside of Sydney, in New South Wales, Australia, so it's going to be: *New South Waves— Hotel & Aquatic Center*. The domain has been secured (thanks, GoDaddy). It's not my finest work, but it's got PJ's essence all over it. He's been researching our loan options.

"I've got a lead on financing! Mates Rates!"

•

I fire up my weathered iMac. I'm pretty sure this is not gonna work. But I miss Shawna's voice.

Dearly.

Enough to give it a try. Keeping secrets from PJ has made me feel lonely and isolated.

Yo?

Hey!

This works? Shawna?

Hello George ;)

No way.

Welcome to the party.

This is pretty cool. It even does the
capitalization thing for you.

It's called the Internet?

Aren't you a Mac owner?! Jesus.

Reluctantly, yes. CONGRATS on school! That
is so wonderful! What do you want for
your graduation gift?

To have you come home?

Ugh.

I know, I know. But I would like
to see you. I miss you.

I know. Me too.

But I DO NOT miss exchanging
sexy emails with you and then
having you disappear. NOT COOL.

Understood. I'm not 100% at fault, you
know. You need to accept some of the
blame. Fair?

Fair. I accept 91%. So, what's her name?

Jesus.

It's OK. I'm cool.

Oh, man. It was Andrea.

Whirlwind over a few days.

Had a boyfriend, 3 years.

> What a bitch! Ugh, god.
>
> I wish I hadn't asked.
>
> I'd like to think that I'm
>
> not jealous. But let's not
>
> do that again. Yuck.

Now you know what it feels like.

No offense.

> Ooof. Ouch. OK. Fair again.
>
> Jesus Fucking Christ. Let's not
>
> do this again. I AM SORRY. OK?
>
> Let it rest.

I'm sorry. Weeelll, not really.

Maybe a tiny bit? It feels good and

horrible to be on the other side for

once. But fair. Let's move on.

> Thank you. Hell hath no fury
>
> like a George…

Enough. Truce?

> Truce. Absolutely.

Anyway, in other news, PJ and I

are kinda looking at a piece of

property here.

> WHAT?

I know, it sounds crazy. But it's pretty doable.

You should see it. I'll try to send some pics.

    (...)—(she starts typing, erases and starts over).

    Were you serious about me coming there?

    I know you were just being nice. But I can't

    help but think about it. I am SO BORED.

    And I miss you. Just being around you.

Yeah, our love/hate relationship

has an addictive element to it.

I hate to admit it but

me too. I miss you, but it pisses

me off. I wasn't just being nice.

I wouldn't say that and not mean

it.

    Really?

Yes. Of course you can come.

We have a foldout couch now,

so it can be a clean separation.

    I can't stay in your bed? WTF???

Uhhh, you can? How scandalous you are!

    Hee-hee.

OK. OK. But also, to be crystal clear—

I can't do a 4th break-up.

Seriously. I can't do it again.

OK?

    No, no, understood. We're not gonna

start dating again. Don't worry.

But I just achieved this huge thing

in my life, and you were such

a big part of it. I wanna close it out

with you. No one makes me laugh like you do.

Primarily because you're so dark and

fucked up. But it's still true. Take it as

a compliment?

Go fuck yourself. But, compliment

accepted. And, if you come, you

have to remember to be nice. Really

nice, OK? Not nice for one second

then pretzel me with psycho-babble

jujitsu moves, OK? Swear on it.

 I AM! I WILL! I SWEAR!

 I just want to see you. OK?

 I really need to see you.

 Goddamnit! I hate it when I'm needy!

Shawna. Listen. I would love

you to come. Come.

OK? Flights are cheap,

anyway—off-season.

Try to arrive on

a Thursday or a Sunday,

so you can take the direct

flight from PTY.

Are you sure?

I'm fucking sure!

OK! Maybe my dad has miles…

All dads have miles. Otherwise no one
under 30 would have a passport.

HA! I need to run. I'm so excited!

(and thank you, George)

Maybe get a blood test, just in case?

Hee-hee. Bye!

Jesus. OK. Bye.

She's the only woman in the world that can give you a boner over
five words via text. "Maybe get a blood test…" is Shawna's euphemism
for "If I'm gonna fly 5,000 miles, we will be having sex."

Heartbreaker.

7

Your girlfriend cheats on you. How do you respond?

a)   Stalk the guy, making endless insecure comparisons between you and him.

b)   Attempt to stay with her and fail.

c)   Move out of the country.

d)   All of the above.

Lately, The Wreck has a weird energy. It's off-season, but it feels pronounced. I still have my shifts, but I'm usually the only guy on, plus a little security. The low season means no DJ. I almost miss the douchey gringos and *Girls Gone Wild* crew. It might be that I'm preoccupied, moonlighting as a junior varsity spy. Tough call.

Primo lives here now. Yesterday, I went to stock some beer, walked into the dry storage and he pulled a boat tarp over a stack of those rectangular boxes. There are at least fifty now. He barked.

"Qué paso?"

"Nada. Estoy almacenamiento la barra." Stocking the bar is my job, bro.

He shooed me with a flick of his hand, pushed me out and locked the door. Raúl must've forgotten to tell him that I have a key to that door.

Fine by me.

Those crates of Balboa are heavy.

Who needs four dozen machine guns? Maybe Tsvika is justified in keeping an eye on him.

It's a quiet night. Primo and I make peace, and I play *Buena Vista Social Club* from my iPod. The oversized speakers from The Wreck pound the bass into your chest. So good.

"Te gustas?" You like it?

"Canciones hermosas." Beautiful music. Who knew Primo was such a lover?

I swim home. The boys are in the kitchen. What a picture-perfect dysfunctional family we make.

"Georgie! Toss'em a Balbie, Tsviks?" Yes, we drink every day. Thank god I only had three beers at work.

"Do we have vodka? Let's not let those fresh limes go to waste." Fresh limes cost a premium and are only available once a month here.

"That's a good mate!"

Tsvika does not like this complication.

"No beer?"

"I've got it, dude. Do you want one?"

"Eh. Vodka? A small one?"

"I do! Huge one!" I slice up the limes. They really are a treat. And they kill whatever giardia is in the ice—made from the filtered water that is not really that filtered.

Tsvika fondles his glass and looks pensive. I need to figure out a subtle way to get him alone.

"Aw, mate! You're not gonna belieeeve this." He runs to his room and returns with his laptop. It's open to the TTTS Facebook page. He's really done a nice job with it.

"It looks great, man. I like how you tightened up the logo. Sweet."

"Loook! Someone donated to the TiTTieS!

"Please stop calling it that."

But he's right. Total donations are up to $943.

"Who kicked in a hundo?"

"Well give us a scroll! Your girl! Portland!"

Whoa.

Stumptown Coffee Company donated $100 and posted:

Great cause! Keep up the good work!

"Wow."

"She paid the toll, ay? Did she evah."

We pound our drinks. One of PJ's big theories (besides getting blown in the shower while eating mint chip ice cream, which actually sounds fantastic) is that if you sleep with someone, you've gotta pay the toll. Normally, it's the guy who pays. Sometimes it's guilt. Sometimes it's a ride to the airport. Sometimes it's a hundred bones, especially when you have…a boyfriend.

"Huh. That's really nice. Kinda classy, right?" Smart of her to launder it through Stumptown, too. I'm sure her boyfriend double-checks her Facebook page. Beautiful, funny, smart, charismatic little cheater.

"You're a bloody gigolo!"

Tsvika finds all of this boring. He finishes his drink and heads to his room without a word. Smooth as silk, that one.

"I'm gonna shower."

"Alright, but don't spend all night, ay? I've got *Gallipoli* cued up! None of that messaging with Shawna fah hours." He must be homesick. He only owns three Aussie movies on his computer, and he watches them every few months. PJ knows that Shawna is coming out. They get along great, but…

When I first came here, I was renting a room by the week. I met PJ downtown—he really has been the best roommate I've ever had—and we subleased an apartment. Shawna came out shortly after. We'd "agreed not to date" until I came back, but she had already booked her ticket. We fought and had sex and fought. So, PJ is a little protective of me, when it comes to Shawna.

I hit the power on my computer. I need to talk to Tsvika, but he beats me to the punch.

Two knocks at my door.

"George?"

"Cruise in, Tsviks. What's up?"

"So today? You see Raúl? At work?"

"No, no Raúl. But, I did see a two thousand percent increase in the gun boxes. They're stacked to the fucking ceiling in the storage room. Maybe it's not so absurd that you're watching him."

"This room? You have access?"

"Uhhh, yeah?"

"One minute."

He returns with the most inelegant looking electronic device I've ever seen.

"Did you steal my dad's first car phone from the '90s?"

He doesn't bite.

"Satellite tracking GPS. This one more reliable than cellular network-based one. Battery last one month."

"Um, cool? You don't have a Q like James Bond? Because this GPS looks more like Janky Bond, than *007*."

"Eh?"

"Ugh. Never mind. I'm just saying—don't you have access to satellite surveillance? That thing seems a little...dated. Right?"

Silence.

"Tsvika, just..."

"With the rifle? Can you get it in the box? Together?"

"Maybe. I dunno. First, can you please answer two direct questions? One: are you or are you not a Mossad agent? Two: why do you care? I mean, Raúl is no Gandhi, but this seems like small potatoes. It doesn't make sense."

"Not important. You work for him. Either you help me or you helping him."

"Tsvika. Seriously. You cannot think that I am involved in any of this shit. Come on."

"You go to Colombia. You watch the boy. Is simple. George, you help, or you are with him."

I'm not sure whether or not I have a choice. Or how I feel. Or if I'll do it. But I waited too long in line to see the *A Team* remake to not at least be curious. And I know what Raúl is up to is bad news. So I listen.

Tsvika breaks it down. Stick it in a box, toward the top of the stack but not the very top of the stack.

He can tell when the box has been moved more than two meters. Impressive. Just think if they used an iPhone, instead of this 1989 Nokia prototype.

He turns for the door. I turn back to my computer. I keep waiting to hear my own voice say, "Fuck this. This is insane. I'm out."

But I don't.

From: Shawna B.

To: Georgeous

Subject: I'M COMING!

Attachment: ExpediaItinBOC.pdf

No, dirtbag, not in that way! I'm coming to Bocas! My flight stuff is below.

Papa B. didn't have miles, but I found an incredible deal on Expedia.

You WILL pick me up, right?

See you soon!

XX

Shawna

PS Blood test status? Just in case…

PPS Dick dick dick dick dick dick dick…

Shawna is allergic to latex. Therefore, condoms are not an option. We have to be pretty frank about our dalliances. She told me that she fucked the other guy with a lambskin condom. Another charming detail I have rattling around in my brain.

From: Georgeous

To: Shawna B.

Subject: my blood test is attached, turbo

Attachment: Lewis_G_sange1131.pdf

i may be an asshole, but I'm a reliable asshole. my blood work is clean. can you say the same? my potassium levels are a bit worrisome, though. too many fried plantains?

healthcare costs are a bargain here in bocas. not unlike underfunded obamacare plus the odd mistaken amputation.

yes, i will pick you up. i promise i will be there, but if anything happens, call my local cell or just cab to the wreck deck (el barco hundido) and ask for jorge—anyone there can find me.

but I will be waiting for you at the airport.

excited to see you (a painful admission).

g

ps in spanish, "i'm coming!" (for girls) is "corriendo!" literally—i'm running! meaning the love juice is running down your leg. leave it to español to keep it street. in french it is?

pps if you have time, please bring me the smallest most expensive waterproof flashlight from REI, whatever batteries it takes and some books. anything. I hate to admit it, but oprah's book club is legit. don't judge. i am a sensitive west coast male through and through. aka cali pussy (your term).

•

Did I run out a few days ago and get a blood test? Yes. Is it 100% conclusive with the Andrea overlap? No. The doctor said a few weeks is more than sufficient, even though the literature always beats the six months drum. Ugh.

I walk out and scan the cupboard for popcorn. In Bocas, they sell the old school kind, where you have to pop the kernels in a pan.

If PJ is homesick tonight, he'll be stoked.

"Awww, mate! You've got the poppies going, ay? Nice one! Do we have buttah?"

PJ's stomach is ripped into oblivion, yet he eats like a kid spending his allowance at 7-11.

"I think so. Check the fridge? I need to keep this thing from burning the house down." *POP POP POP*. He walks over and whispers to me.

"The Tsviks? He's IN! Said his family wants to invest!"

"Really? Why? Because of the airport access? His family is really in the real estate business?" I don't know that I'm ecstatic about comingling my miniature nest egg with Tsvika, only to continue on as his confidential informant.

"Piece of cake! And think about it! Zero worries about security! I told'em the mangy beast has to come with!" I look at Wiglaf to weigh in.

Nothing.

Maybe Wiglaf has a GPS embedded in his collar.

"You've got a point." He does. "Let's watch the movie."

"Mellie G is a legend in this one!" He's right. Mel Gibson kills it in *Gallipoli*.

But he also dies.

From: Shawna B.

To: Georgeous

Subject: Le petit mort

That's what they call it in French—the small death. Clever, huh?

I got your flashlight. It is SO small. And not cheap! There is no way it can possibly float. Whatever. You're worth it. We'll call it a late (very late) 29th birthday present. Besides the one I'm already bringing you. See you in two days!!!

XX

Shawna

PS Yes, I got blood tested too. I may be a bitch, but I'm a self-aware bitch :)

Today's to do list: place the super spy GPS.

"Want a Gatorade? I'm gonna hit the Chino." PJ came with me into town. He has to go to the bank.

The Chino, or Las Tiendas Chinas, is what they call the convenience stores/bodegas, since they're all Chinese-owned. The slang is terrible, but as previously mentioned, we're all about timesaving. Half of the time, I pay them in soaking wet dollar bills. They don't even flinch. In the Caribbean, money is money, wet or not.

"For sure. Could it get any hotter? Lemon-lime or orange, please."

"Gotcha. Hey, fancy a stubbie holdah?"

"Absolutely. If they have them? Buy them all." Beer koozies are gold here, because beer gets warm so quickly. It's a little hillbilly, but it's not uncommon to whip one out at a decent restaurant. Yet another reason why the Caribbean, and Panama especially, is so enchanting.

While he shops, I reach a sweaty palm into the pocket of my shorts, to feel where the GPS left an imprint on my thigh. I decided to leave it in the Minnow, for now. I want to try to place it today, on the way back with Shawna. I'd give anything to come clean to PJ. But I can't. Anxiety-filled sweating shall continue. Plus, it's 95 degrees today.

PJ returns, and I suck my drink down. Anti-freeze colored or not, Gatorade is delicious.

He holds out the koozies.

"Pick one!" They are beautiful, both red with white lettering. *Yo* ♥ *Panama* and *PANAMANIAC!!!* There's really no choice, yo.

"You are joking." He acquiesces and hands me the *Yo* ♥ *Panama* one. "No PanaMamacita for Shawna?"

"Careful with that one. She's a heartbreakah. Don't go making PanaBabies when you are rooting each othah into oblivion tonight." He's referencing how loud Shawna can be when we have sex. Even though I'm accustomed to it, sometimes his frankness catches me off guard. I burst into laughter.

"PJ, you're so cute when you're righteous. Any other guidance?"

"Aw, have a real go, mate!"

"Thanks for the koozie. It's fantastic."

"They are nice, ay? It was fate! The last two!" He points to *PANAMANIAC!!!* and gives a psychopathic grin.

"Amazing. Hey, you're staying in town, right? I'll walk you to the bank and then head up to the airport."

"Giddy up!"

We pass the owner of The Casbah and wave. He's eating street food from the cart that's permanently parked in front of The Bookstore. The Bookstore does sell books, but it also sells drinks and closes every night at 2am—even on Mondays. He shares a few scraps from his plate with one of the abundant stray dogs in Bocas. Shawna would adopt them all.

A gringo walks towards us and eyes PJ. His clothes say he lives here, but his lack of a tan suggests otherwise. He's either a part-time resident or comes often, because someone else in his life is. Like his wife. I check his ring finger.

Yep.

With his eyes locked on PJ, I have a chance to check him out. He looks studious, like William Hurt from the *Accidental Tourist*. But his beefy frame says he could do some damage. And PJ looks like he's got his hand in the cookie jar.

We've been here a long time. Everyone knows PJ. It's not

uncommon for someone to stop him on the street and say, "Hey! You
gave me a surf lesson last week!" It's also not uncommon for someone
to stop him and ask, "Hey! Did you give my wife a surf lesson last
week?" The silence that follows says it all.

William Hurt passes without incident. I triple check his ring finger.

"Who was that?"

"Who?"

"The guy that just walked by. Old school Hawaiian shirt, new
school revenge in his eyes?"

"Oh, the oldie? Dunno."

"Are you sure? You've got nothing?"

"Ay? The heat has really gotten you off your rockah, mate."

"Never mind." I don't have the energy to argue.

It's ten times hotter in town than on our little island of Carenero.
The black paved streets jack the heat up. Mondays are garbage days,
but this week must've been a holiday, because the streets are disgusting.

"Do you smell a fiyah?" I don't. All I can think about is that a GPS
device, possibly sanctioned by the Israeli government, is bobbing up
and down in the S.S. Minnow. The thought of it is giving me a panic
attack. Tsvika told me that it's waterproof—that's pretty cool.

"It must be the fincas. I think they're burning all of the old cane in
the fields."

"Uh, it's awful. And check out the rubbish! These wankers bettah
not let it float over to our posh pad at Bluff!"

"No kidding." The trash problem here is catastrophic. In the next
ten years, this place will either become the next Saint Martin or the

next Tijuana. Remaining in between is not sustainable.

By the time we get to the bank, I wanna crawl inside a freezer. It wasn't long ago that I met Andrea here, and I was planning our life together. Now I'm about to have a repeat of nearly all the same experiences, with Shawna. There's really not that much to do in Bocas. That's why people come here. But the swapping sensation feels surreal and tasteless.

"If you meet a girl in line, who is wearing a novelty t-shirt, don't hit on her. Trust me."

"Ay?"

"Never mind. See you back at the ranch."

"Bloody hell, it's hot! Race yah to be the first one to move their bed into an Esky of piss!" Beers on ice do sound dreamy.

"And now we have plans for tonight. Beers on ice. *A Man, a Plan, a Canal, Panama.*"

We both smile. Me at my unoriginal, overplayed palindrome, PJ at any mention of cold beer.

Too bad a tiny bag of ice costs $5.

•

It's only 11:30am, but I have to get a beer. My t-shirt smells like a men's softball team. There's a dark, windowless sports bar across the street from the airport.

And they have air conditioning.

Hallelujah.

I order a beer and pop it into the koozie. The bartendress giggles at me. Crazy gringos.

Shawna's plane lands on the tiny airstrip. At night, kids come out here and practice their batting, when the grownups have taken over the adjacent baseball field. I've really got to come see Giovani play again.

The ten second walk to the airport is blistering.

"HI!"

"Hi, sweetie." We hug and kiss. The kisses are cordial. The hugs are not.

"Dead serious: how do you get more beautiful every time I see you?" She really does.

"Shut up!"

"Swear on my life."

"Awww. Thank you. You're sooo tan! Fuck, it's hot! This place makes LA feel like the Arctic."

"I know. Today is especially bad. The farms are burning their fields off. Let's have a quick beer in the AC. I'm gonna see if I can get someone to pick us up. Walking more is not an option."

"I'd kill for a cold Diet Coke." We exit the teeny airport, walk across the street, sit and order drinks. It's such a treat to look into her eyes. Even walking a few steps, we have a certain…I don't know…cadence. Her familiarity is intoxicating.

"I forgot how dense the jungle is when you fly over! It looks like a stack of broccoli at the farmer's market!"

"Great description." I grab our drinks. My homegirl nods at the koozie's second debut. I'll have to tip her an extra buck, for stroking my ego.

"I think she likes you!"

"Nah. I was just in here twenty minutes ago. She seems friendly, and I think she is, but you never know."

"She's not friendly?"

"That's not what I mean. She is, probably. The problem with trying to decipher a second language is that you're so busy translating in your head that you miss the subtle nuances. For example, when I was just focusing on understanding her mumble of 'Do you want something to drink?', her eyes might have been saying, 'Fuck you, imperialist.'"

"Jesus. I can see your biting cynicism has traveled well."

"Sorry. I'll wait until you've been here a full hour, before I unleash the dark side."

"Deal."

Shawna frantically flips through her phone.

"Oh my god! I've got to show you something!"

She starts talking crazy fast, like a maniac. Not quite like a *PANAMANIAC!!!* but close.

"I stayed with my mom the last two nights, so she could take me to the redeye at LAX. I've been so bored post dissertation, I tackled decluttering her dining room. It's become consumed by her 'art,' also known as all the shit she buys from Michaels."

She finds it and presses her phone against her chest, building it up.

"It's absurd, right? A completely impossible task. So I flip through one of her creations. She has made a fucking scrapbook of your articles. All of them!"

"No way."

"Look!" I look. It's legit. Puffy pen writing, cursive, everything sprinkled with glitter.

"That's your quiz from the mid-October piece. I like that one about the appropriate amount of post-coital cuddling."

"You really read them all, too, eh?" I'm crazy flattered. "Is that my name with sequins glued on top of it?"

"Those are called 'dazzle buttons'. Don't judge. It's my mom." She takes a sip of her Diet Coke. "Of course I read all of your stuff!"

My beer is almost gone. I text Giovani. It's only a $2 trip to the boat. It's not really worth his while—but I hook him up with every single tourist that comes to the bar—so he takes care of me.

---

en cam

Giovani—you complete me.

Ten minutes later, I see him round the corner. I couldn't be happier to see his pickup.

He drives right by us.

He thinks another white dude fifteen feet away is me. All of you gringos look the same, man.

I know, dude. We think so, too.

The few steps to his pickup feel like we're walking inside an oven. So hot.

I heave Shawna's bag into the truck bed, and we hop in. He takes us the twelve blocks to The Wreck. $1.80. I give him $5.

Giovani's life is so simple. I'm envious. But only because I don't really know him.

"This is where you work?"

When she first came out, I hadn't gotten this gig. PJ and I had were still in our little apartment, before landing at Tsvika's.

"Yeah, pretty cool, huh?"

"Very cool!"

"Oye, Flacito." Raúl's in a good mood, calling me by my nickname, Skinny.

"Raúl, Shawna."

"Mucho gusto, bella." Nice to meet you, beautiful. He either likes what he sees or is reconfirming that I'm not a maricón—aka homosexual.

Probably both.

Fucking macho criminal.

Shawna touches me in a very familiar way. I don't stop her.

"Hola! Nice to meet you!" She speaks zero Spanish, but she has one of those smiles that brings the house down.

It's so good to see her.

"Placer." My pleasure? Back off, Raúl. Get your own chica. Too bad I'm going to sell her smile down the river to place the GPS.

I walk Shawna's bag over to the Minnow and carefully set it in. Damn, it's heavy.

I snag the GPS, wrap it in a Speedo and slide it into my pocket. Its bulk makes my shorts sway, like a pocketful of tokens at the batting cages.

It's now or never.

"Uh, uno Diet Coke, por favor?"

"Por su puesto, mi reina." Of course, my queen? Raúl thinks he's on a fucking date. But I may as well milk it. I see him grab the Abuelo, to give her drink a little kicker.

"Raúl, mi otro traje de baño? Has visto?" It's a weak cover, but I'm positive he couldn't give a shit about where my fourth missing Speedo is.

"No sé." He responds while ogling Shawna's tits.

Fucker.

It's go time. One last glance around the bar for a surprise visit from Primo and I head to the dry storage.

I stick my key into the door and fake-wipe the sweat off my brow, allowing a side glance to see if Raúl is concerned.

Nope.

I can feel my heart in my throat, but as soon as I pull the GPS out of my pocket, my movements become mechanical.

Door unlock. Close door. It auto-locks. Shove case of Balboa across door but just an inch—for a three-second insurance policy. Power up the GPS. Climb rack. Grab gun box. Slide out. Open. Place the GPS. Replace box like Jenga piece. Reverse all steps.

Let's be honest—I'm killing it.

Climbing down the racks, I hear the distinct jangle of empty beer bottles in a plastic crate. They are worth twenty cents apiece, as a deposit, and not to be thrown away.

My eyes lock on the door. I try to climb down the last few rungs without looking.

Mistake.

Sweat and anxiety are not my friends.

Clank clank clank clank.

SLAM.

I hit the floor in the fetal position.

I hear a chiropractic adjustment in my spine, which feels oddly good, as I lie on the floor.

In a single motion, I break-dance-kick the empty Balboa case out of the way and pull the Speedo from my pocket. Holding it in the air, it looks like I'm an outfielder showing the umpire that I caught the ball.

The umpire steps in.

"Qué paso?"

I respond pathetically, panting, as Raúl sets the bottles down.

"Esta…ariba…secando." I point the Speedo toward the single vent in the room that has a latch to control the shutters. Lucky for my stupid ass, it's both a logical place to dry a Speedo and also to fall from.

Raúl laughs in disgust.

"Próxima vez? Afuera." Next time? Dry it outside, dumbfuck.

Phew.

I walk out, rubbing the Speedo against my soon-to-be bruised shoulder.

"What happened?"

"I fell, trying to grab this from the vent. I stuck it up there to dry."

A few empty shot glasses accompany her Diet Coke. I'm thankful to Raúl for entertaining her, but his lusting eyes tell that me he didn't do it for me.

But the success of my mission (doesn't that sound awesome?)

calms me. I can see the flirty booze in Shawna's eyes. She reaches out and fingers my Speedo, like it's lingerie.

"Well, we'll just have to get you another one now, won't we!?"

Raúl, in his most gracious moment of all time (and to impress Shawna), pours me two shots of Abuelo and each of them one.

"Toma. Aspirina." Rum—the Bocas Tylenol.

"Salud." We take them down. They work.

I turn to Shawna.

"We should motor, before it gets too late." I catch Raúl in the eyes, deferential, to smooth our exit. "Raúl, gracias."

"Con cuidate, mono." Be careful, monkey? Is he fucking with me? That was either a clever metaphor for my climbing skills, a warning or a sexual innuendo. But I'm certainly not going to ask him to clarify.

I help Shawna off the barstool. Confirmed—she is drunk.

Thanks to the combined weight of us and her luggage, the S.S. Minnow nearly does a wheelie. Two hundred feet out on the water, the ocean air feels like a gift from god. Cool. Peaceful. Safe.

I'm not cut out for this *Spy Game* bullshit.

"Hey, I know you think you're the dog whisperer, but be careful around Wiglaf. I've never seen him bite, at least not a human, but he's got much more of the trained guard dog vibe. Maybe don't do that sharing your ice cream cone thing with him. He might bite your hand off."

"Anyone who names their dog after a Beowulf character had a bad childhood."

"WOOOGHF." Great comedic timing, Wiglaf.

We pull up at our dock.

"Are you kidding! This is your place? It's INCREDIBLE!"

A case of beer, in bottles, weighs thirty-five pounds. Her luggage? Easily sixty.

"What do you have in here?"

"Worry about your own luggage. Hey, can I shower?"

"Of course. I'm gonna jump in the water, anyway. Let's get you set up." Wiglaf is sitting in his version of relaxed Indian style—on his hind legs, erect, stone-faced as a gargoyle.

"That is the scariest dog I've ever seen. Can I pet him?"

"Yeah, let me introduce you, first." I give him my fist, which he moves half an inch to sniff, then he returns to sentry mode. I take Shawna's hand and do the same. She pets him lightly, and then scratches his ears.

"Who's a good boy, eh? Such a good boy…" He wags his tail! Kidding. But he does sort of swish it to the other side. Thanks a lot, bro.

"Come on. Let's go. If I don't cool down, I'm gonna freak out."

"OK. OK."

I already have towels laid out for her.

"Such the host. Thank you!"

"Bathroom's in there. Go crazy."

"I LOVE YOUR PLACE! No wonder you don't want to leave!" Her vibrancy transforms my uninspired room for the better.

I drop my clothes and grab my trunks. Shawna looks at my love hammer, unabashedly. It's swollen from the thought of her showering.

"Already?! Jeez!"

"You *are* drunk."

"I'm on vacation!"

"That's fair." She looks back at my cock. "Hey, look away! I'm just putting on my swimsuit, pervert." But I'm glad she doesn't. "I hope shampoo/conditioner/body wash all-in-one works. PJ might have something fancier for his hair."

"I brought my own, thank you. Go. Go get in the water." But she teases me by stripping down to her bra, on her way to the bathroom.

Fucker.

Walking into the kitchen, a stroke of genius hits. I stick a Balboa can in my new koozie, soak the koozie in water and stick the whole thing in the freezer.

I love thinking of Shawna puttering around my room, putting on hand cream and deciding which of her forty-five sundresses to wear.

She's got a whole lotion series post-shower. I've got time.

I kick off my flip-flops, saunter into the water and swim out to the middle of our bay. It's about fifteen feet deep, and I can see all the way to the bottom. An old cordless phone acts as an artificial reef for two starfish. It's a bummer, but it's a little perfect, too. I see PJ coming in on a boat-taxi and wave.

"Georgie! You're barely visible out here! We almost nicked yah!"

"I'm good, man. I keep my eyes out."

"You havin' a propah swim, or do you wanna come back with me?

"I'll hop in. Shawna's probably out of the shower by now."

PJ pulls me into the boat. The driver doesn't even blink at a gringo hitching a ride and drenching his boat's floor.

"Why aren't you joining her?"

"Easy." I look at his board. "Where'd you go?"

"Wizards."

"Good?"

"It was pretty glassy, but some local bloke kept cutting me off!
Wanted to rip his head off."

The territorialism of surfing is such a buzzkill.

"Be careful, man. You probably deflowered his sister. He might be
looking for revenge. Be safe. You're way outnumbered, and those guys
will knife you, no joke." I pause and look him in the eye. "No more
local girls, OK? And I'm not just talking about Panamanian girls, the
white ones, too. If they live here, don't fuck them. There are plenty of
tourists to prey on. We're trying to set up shop here." Any mention of
potentially committing to the land, and PJ's smile is back.

"Ah, mate. I promise to be a good boy! But this heat! It makes me
feel like an old geezah! I could drink a liter of piss."

"Well, I have a present for you. In the freezer. I soaked the koozie
in water and stuck the beer in with it. I figure the koozie will freeze
before the beer. Voila! Ice cold beer. Albeit a bit messy when it melts."

"Look atch you! Bloody Isaac Newton!"

"How do you even know that?

"Uni. Doesn't mattah. Love yah work!"

PJ pays the driver and grabs his board. I follow him onto the dock,
trying to look nonchalant, in just my Speedo.

Shawna is standing with her feet in the water, sipping a drink.

"Hi!"

"Hiya, sweetheart!" PJ bear-hugs her, off her feet, etc. His ability to pull off cheesiness is limitless.

"I mixed a warm Diet Coke, from my bag, with some of your vodka. I hope that's OK? I don't normally drink this early, but…" Vodka and Coke. Gross. Vanesa's drink of choice. I need to hit the Chino and buy her some juice or soda water.

"Welcome to the club!" PJ looks back at me, then grimaces at my Speedo. "Go put some boardies on! Christ!"

"Freezer. Go." And like a little kid racing down the stairs, he's gone.

"Nice swim?"

"It was great."

"I met Shveetcha?"

"Close. It's pronounced 'Sveekuh'."

"He had two guys with him, but as soon as I said hello, they went down to his room. Then, two minutes later, they came back upstairs and took off."

"Don't take it personally. His social skills are…"

"Lacking?"

"Exactly. I think they hole up in his room and play those networked video games—where you role-play mercenaries or counter-intelligence agents or something."

I find joking in these half-truths stress relieving.

"Isolationist. Sounds like a perfect roommate."

"Agree to agree."

"Hey, is your shoulder OK? You must've fallen pretty hard."

"I fell on my own stupidity. Not a soft landing."

Her tender concern makes my eyes wander.

"Are you looking at my tits?"

"Yeah, sorry. I can't help it. You look incredible." She sways, appreciative of the attention.

"You, too. Where did all those muscles come from?" I'm still skinny as a rail, but I'll take it. "Come on. Come check out your stuff!"

We pass PJ. He's just finished the frozen koozie/beer concoction.

"Mate! She's a beauty! We should get a patent!" He's already trying it with his *PANAMANIAC!!!* koozie.

"Save me one?"

"'Course!"

Shawna and I head to my room.

"Huh? One what?"

"I froze the koozies for PJ."

"Oh! Smart!" She takes a reluctant sip of her drink. "Hey, this tastes awful. Later can we get some…"

"Juice or something? Of course. Whatever you want." Vanesa guilt? Adios.

In my room, she has it all laid out. Three books. The dopest flashlight I've ever seen and…a new Speedo, with the American flag on it.

Ridiculous.

I grab the flashlight first.

"I'm not convinced that it floats, but the Navy Seals use those!"

"Shawna. It's perfect. It's so small—I can keep it in my pocket. Let's do a quick test!" I fill up the sink with water. It seems like a waste, but the water quality here is terrible.

It floats. Crazy.

"Oh my god! How does it do that?" I kiss her. Then I really kiss her. She gasps.

"Ahmmm." Her body softens to my touch.

"Wait! Try on the Speedo!"

"Now?"

"Yes, now! It's supposed to remind you of your homeland, idiot."

"OK." I take off the one I have on and put it on. Shawna checks its status with her eyes. No shame. The red stripes do provide a nice accent to my package.

"Should I grow a moustache?"

"Hee-hee."

"So wrong."

"So right!"

"I feel unusually patriotic."

She reaches for me.

We fumble at first, but within a minute, I'm inside her.

"Ahhh. You feel like…"

She moans.

"Bliss. You, too." But that's not what I mean. She feels like…home. We fuck like greased puzzle pieces. She is not quiet. I want to shush her, but I can't. Each gasp makes me feel like a hero. It's so thoughtless and fluid. I have to pull away from her to come, just so I can see her. We've been at it for what, a year? OK, probably twenty minutes, but seeing her tits jostle makes me go.

We catch our breath.

"Saving it up for me?"

"Yeah, sorry, I just…god, you feel amazing."

"No, I love it."

We kiss a little. I clean her up.

"Would you mind getting me something to drink? I can't move. My legs are numb."

"For sure. Be right back."

I throw on shorts and head to the kitchen, to ice down two waters. Fuck.

Marco is there, on the edge of our porch, chucking rocks. There is no way he did not hear us. I open the door, walk out and see his target. He's dismantling a mid-sized lizard from a short distance. The poor lizard's back right leg is broken.

"MARCO!" He's holding a rock in the air, poised for another amputation. "Dámelo!" Busted. He hands it to me. "Venga!"

I grab his arm. He resists a little but stands at my side next to the lizard. I look him in the eyes. Then, in one fatal blow, I put the lizard out of its misery. Its lukewarm blood sprays my leg and hits Marco in the arm. I pick him up and sit him on the porch—maybe a little too hard.

"Esperate!" It's the first time I've ever seen him afraid of me. I go into the kitchen and grab four plastic bags, from our last trip to the Chino. I hand them to him.

"Doscientas piezas de basura. Ahora!" He looks up and can tell that I'm not budging. Two hundred pieces of trash sounds like a lot, but it's not. He obeys. I take the water to Shawna.

"That was…"

"Untoppable. Hey, sorry. Marco is here? And I think he heard us?"

"Oh, my god! I'm sorry! Was I too loud?"

"It doesn't matter. He needs a little parental supervision right now. Is that cool?"

"Of course, go!"

"He was torturing a baby lizard, about as long as your pinky."

"No!"

"Yes. Little tyrant. I made him pick up two hundred pieces of trash."

"Two hundred?"

"Relax. Around here? Fifteen minutes, tops. Any tide pool will yield a quick fifty."

"You're tough. But it's a good punishment. Endorsed!"

"Cool. But come up in a bit, OK? If he finishes, I'll swim with him. He'll freak at the new flashlight."

I walk out and watch Marco. He's dragging his feet, but he's doing it. A bit later, Shawna walks out, carrying my trunks, a towel, the flashlight and what PJ has apparently named the, "Eskoozie." Brilliant.

I pop the beer. I'm glad we're not dating anymore. She looks hot enough to inspire a generation of divorce attorneys.

Marco comes back. There's stuff in all four bags. They're not completely full, but it's still impressive. I'm wondering if my punishment was a little light.

"Contarlos."

The request doesn't faze him. He starts counting.

"Veinte uno, veinte dos." Before he hits forty, I realize that he may not know how to count to two hundred. He's never in school. I rethink this add-on as possibly cruel and unusual punishment.

"Bastante. En la basura." He knows our compound better than I do. I don't have to tell him where the trash is. He comes back to my side but doesn't look me in the eyes.

Shawna spectates. As a child guardian, she's tough as nails. But she can only do it for three minutes before the endless hugging, kissing and second round of desserts comes out.

He eyes the swimming stuff. Not so easy, little man. I take off my watch, set my timer and hand it to him.

"Por ahí. En la silla. Con silencio. Va." He goes. Ten minutes of silence is kitten food to him. Silence is his bit. But I want to send a message.

"Wow, your Spanish sounds pretty good."

"That's just because you don't know any. That probably sounded like, 'Marco, you make the trash of the upset I am, sitting with your silence.' Thank you for the beer."

"Ha! You're welcome. Why does PJ call them Eskoozies?"

"Because Esky is an Australian brand of coolers. An 'Esky of piss' is a cooler full of beer."

"Is that racist?"

"No, it's just Australian. Eskoozie is genius, but PJ's got it like that.”

"I like it! Rolls off the tongue. PJ does have something going on. If he were a painting, he'd be a Rothko. So simple, but you could stare at it for hours."

"Exactly." I stare into her eyes. She drops a smile like an atomic bomb.

I'm fucked.

I remind myself that she's probably still in touch with him—her UCLA side guy. He likely sends her dirty texts from his new associate professor job in Bozeman. Yes, I stalk him online. This cracks my current façade of her perfection.

Shatters it.

Beep beep beep. The watch alarm is done. Marco looks at me but stays seated.

"Venga." He comes. "Mi amiga, Shawna."

"Hiii, Marco!"

"Hola." He's not quite there.

"Qué dices?" What did you say (aka—address her with respect)?

"Hola, señora. Mucho gusto." I move my hand up, instructing him to shake hers. He does it, and it's so damn cute.

"Tienes gafas?" He pulls his goggles out of his pocket. Charming little trouble-maker. "Vamonos."

I do a quick deck change, swig my beer while it's still cold and head out with him. Being a disciplinarian fits me poorly, and I give up Jortuga in about eight seconds. He smiles. It must be so fulfilling to be a parent. And exhausting.

We get out of the water, for a little break. Shawna brings drinks. She found the Quik. This woman knows what she's doing. I'm pretty spent, but one last toy needs some love, and it's already getting dark. That's right—Fetchlight with the new Special Forces-approved torch. I show it to Marco and tell him that it floats, but he's not buying it.

"Qué flota?"

"Sí! Mira!"

I turn it on and shine its beam on a couple of nearby trees. I chuck it but not too far. It weighs nothing. I could've thrown it to the moon. He goes for it. I'm not sure if it's the billions of lumens it's got, or the fact that Marquito can hold it inside his little palm, but the light show is spectacular.

"That is the best overpriced man-toy I've ever seen. Look at him go! It's beautiful, almost psychedelic." We side hug/cuddle together.

A moment of perfection.

Little Marquito looks beat. But I'm sure he'll go again. I reach for the flashlight, and he hands it over. He must be more emotionally tired than anything.

"You did so well! You are such a good swimmer!" Shawna showers him with hugs and hair tousling. She even kisses him on the forehead.

The kicker is—he likes it. He can't understand a word she's saying, but he warms to her, in his shy little way.

Primo shows up.

What?

He slows, as he passes by on an enduro motorcycle. I look at Marco. Then I look at Primo. Everything becomes so simple: teaching kids to swim is good, and trafficking guns is bad.

Primo spots Marco and looks surprised, but then he barks out at him.

"Marco. Casa. Ahora." He acts like he came to tell Marco it's time to go home. This loosely veiled exchange tells me that he's keeping an eye on me.

Beep beep beep.

Not my watch. The sound of the GPS playing in my head.

8

How to keep your girl from cheating on you:

No matter how many times you drive her to the airport, make sure you spend three seconds telling her, "I love you, and I'm gonna miss you."

We lie in bed, after the longest and, possibly, best evening of my life.

"Can we have sex, even if I can't get a hard?"

"Uh, why?"

"I want to be inside you again, so badly. I think I spent my chi, but I still want to feel you. I need it."

"Okaaay. You're so sweet sometimes. And my god, you with Marco. I think I ovulated just watching you with him! Even when he was in trouble, he knew you cared about him so much."

"I dunno."

"No. It's true. With you being gone so long…I've thought about a lot."

"Of course you have. Anyone who sits in front of the computer all day becomes hyper-emotional. It's the predicament of the modern day intellectual laborer."

"Let me finish."

I turn and look at her. She covers up, to help me focus.

"It's never enough. You kept saying that. And you were right. I should've realized that it *was* enough. I was too tough on you—always calling you heady and tormented. But I think, really, you're just curious. Alert. And honest. You're so honest. Almost too honest…with yourself."

Whoa.

Was not expecting this.

"I had dozens of art theory books out in front of me. So much beauty and risk and love. And I…"

"It's really amazing what you did in school. I'm so glad…"

"Let. Me. Finish."

"OK. Sorry."

"That's what you do. You're like an artist. Not that you paint stuff, but you live in the same way. You look, and you see, and you're critical. But in the end, you give it all away. You give everything you have to others. That is your art."

"That's a stretch."

"OK. OK. Let me give you an example. Do you remember when we went to your Aunt's?"

"In Glendora, at Christmas?"

"Exactly. And you were picking on your uncle for being hardcore right-wing, and then on the way home you got annoyed at all of the strip malls paving over paradise…"

"What an asshole."

"Exactly! That's what I thought! What a fucking asshole!"

"Agreed."

"Shush." I do. "But then I replayed it. And I remembered you teasing your aunt and helping her with the dishes. You let your uncle show you all of his tools. ALL of them. You never left me alone for too long. And on the way home, you were hating on LA. The traffic was insane. But, at the same time, you were stroking my knee and playing my favorite playlist."

"The endless dance music one?"

"Yeah, that one. I'm just saying it was enough. I didn't see it, but it was. No one makes me feel like you do. So beautiful. And no one treats me like you do. So loved. Thank you. Thank you, George. You will always be the love of my life."

Under different circumstances, after this onslaught of love and adoration, I might have gotten down on one knee and popped the question. But the only question I really want to ask is: why did you fuck that guy? And, more importantly, why did you tell me about it?

•

Shawna's trip is only ten days, and it's going by quickly. Most nights, we get in bed as early as possible, so we can chat, laugh and spend so much time having sex that I consider shopping for a prosthetic penis on Amazon. Sadly, Amazon Prime does not deliver to Bocas, yet.

I can tell that Shawna is not ecstatic about the Surf & Shag Shack, but she clearly made a commitment to herself to be supportive of me and not to second-guess. I'm curious to know her opinion, but I prefer her silence to her wrath.

The whole thing is as good as done. We're putting in $5k apiece and taking out a loan for $60k more. The land is only $40k, but we need the extra $35k to do most of the building, before we can start bringing in revenue. It doesn't sound like that much money, but we're talking about a piece of dirt next to the jungle that requires four-wheel drive to access. We can walk to the one bar out there, which is cool, and likely to be a side job for me.

PJ has gone absolutely apeshit, printing up the New South Waves—Hotel & Aquatic Center business plan, running the financials, forecasting, etc. He never ceases to amaze. I will not lie. It does feel like a headfirst dive into the deep end of a pool that's just been drained.

PJ has a bank connection that will lend us the remaining $60k. It's at 7.5%, which is decent for a commercial loan. It's a miracle they would lend us anything. Again, this is a piece of dirt. A loan officer at Banco Nacional is going to proxy the paperwork with us today. We should be able to sign the contract tomorrow.

Can I get a Xanax?

Tsvika has told me to keep moving forward with everything—keep my job at The Wreck and keep PJ going on the Surf & Shag Shack. But I'm struggling with what is pretend and what is real, especially when PJ asked us both for our bank routing numbers.

Tsvika finally told me who he works for and what his motivation is for watching Raúl. Just kidding. He hasn't said boo. I wasn't a fan of him insinuating that I am in cahoots with Raúl, so I haven't brought it up again, either. Raúl and Tsvika—two creepy weirdos. Well, they can fucking have each other.

I get out of the shower, and Shawna is fake sleeping. She's usually up, looking at weird art blogs and an entire underworld of fashion websites. They get updated every day; it's insane. Her long morning snooze is passive resistance to this transaction.

I give her a love nudge.

"Good morning. Coffee?"

"Yes, please."

I give her a kiss. Not on her mouth.

"Sure you don't want to come today?"

"Absolutely sure. I want to sit outside in that chair and read my backlog of The Bible." Aka *ELLE* magazine. They weigh three pounds apiece. On the regional flight to Bocas, you have to pay for checked luggage by the kilo, and I know she won't admit to me what she paid in overage. Plus, I think she calls it *The Bible* to make her more approachable to other women. As in, "I just wanna get my nails done and read a magazine!" But the last time I sat next to Shawna while she got a pedicure, she was reading *Margaret Thatcher: The Autobiography* and an article on the psychology of graffiti culture.

Trouble.

Stupidly, I pick up one of her magazines and flip through it.

"How many trees had to die to produce this thing?"

"Why don't you open it and look at the publisher, dick."

I do.

It's Hearst—Publisher of *Esquire*. I can't win.

"Uhm, you're right. I'm wrong. I'm sorry. I'll change?"

I need to use this phrase in one of my *Esquire* vignettes. I'll call it: *How to gracefully end an argument.* The only piece that's missing is the first step—giving up any hope of winning. It's pointless.

"Good boy. Coffee. Go."

I hear PJ, before I round the corner to the kitchen. He is an early riser now and even makes coffee. Everyone is growing up.

"Hey, is there enough left for Shawna?"

"Cooome on, mate! This ain't my first barbeque!"

He grabs her a cup, and I add a little milk and Equal (gross).

"You sorted?"

He has his most provocative t-shirt on: *Marriage—the most expensive way to ruin sex.*

"I'm good. Five minutes."

I drop the coffee. Shawna remains aloof. She leaves tomorrow, and her mood could stem from a number of sources. Separation anxiety? I should ask why, but I don't.

I head back to the kitchen. PJ is already in the Minnow, with Tsvika. I jog out to join them.

"Giddy up!" He starts the Minnow, like a brand-new pencil sharpener. Tsvika is cramped next to me and addresses us.

"We are needing a bigger boat, yes?" I laugh, nervously, hoping his accidental *JAWS* reference is not a bad omen.

Tsvika is cool as a cucumber at The Wreck, but I can feel the GPS's signal beating in my chest. Since I've placed the GPS, my stress-sweat level has gone from "white dude in the tropics" to "did you just take a shower in your clothes?"

It's awful.

I keep looking at Tsvika, almost hoping he panics. He doesn't. Third tier espionage, hopeless real estate investments and putting my girl in the cross hairs of international thugs? It's fucking Bocas.

It's the constant lying to PJ that I hate the most. The guy doesn't have a deceptive bone in his body.

We walk toward the bank in silence. PJ breaks the air with an unusually serious tone. I didn't know he had it in him.

"Tsviks? May I ask you somethin'?"

"Yes."

"What makes you want to do this with us, ay? You have so many other mates. Are you sure you want to do this with us?"

If Tsvika didn't have me under his thumb to take down Raúl, I would've asked the exact same question. Just earlier. Not thirty seconds before we sign our lives away.

"Is good investment. You are good guys. And you leave me alone. No molesting."

Well put. And he's right. I wouldn't molest him.

But prickish anxiety aside, he gave PJ the answer he wanted. That's the exact reason PJ would want him to do it with us. Me, too, honestly. To leave us alone. OK, and also to provide money, technology and security. We are his bro trophy wives. His brophies.

Tsvika does this weird thing with his mouth that I never noticed before, because I rarely saw him. But now that we've been spending more time together, planning doomed real estate ventures and thwarting bad guys, I've witnessed him blowing bubbles with his spit, when he thinks no one is looking.

So disgusting.

There is no way he is running the front desk at the hotel.

We sit down with the bank rep, like underdressed children. She's an attractive woman in her mid-thirties. Her business suit and skirt feel out of place in Bocas. But the brief glimpse of her elegance is refreshing. She gives PJ a subtle, knowing glance.

"Hi. I'm George."

"Nice to meet you." She turns. "Mr. PJ. Nice to see you."

"Hiya!"

She turns to Tsvika. He's distracted, looking at the ceiling. For what? Audio bugs? Ms. Businesswoman shrugs and turns back to PJ, letting loose a quick smile.

Fuck.

Our broker is one of PJ's conquests. I check her ring finger.

Married.

She gives a cursory glance through the documents.

"Gentlemen, everything is in order. One slight delay—the bank didn't finalize the transfer. But it won't be long. Just one more week."

"Anothah week!"

I suppress my relief.

I was not ecstatic to do this when we walked in. And we're not obligated until we sign. Thank god nothing in the world really works. Would you want your cellphone to always work? Always? Everyone wants somewhere to hide, occasionally. And, "Huh, that's weird? I didn't get your text. The cell tower must be down or something." is a much better solution than having to be honest all of the time. "Oh, your text? Yeah, I just didn't respond, because I think you're boring."

We exit.

"PJ! You slept with our loan broker? What the fuck?"

"She's just processing the docs, mate. Relax! Plus she's an attorney!"

"For what, the Panama Papers?"

"Geooorgie. Be nice."

"PJ. Do you understand the concept of a fatal flaw? Because your dick is going to be the end of you. If her husband ever finds out, we're done."

"It's all good! We're sorted! I can't believe we have to wait another week!"

He's right. His carnal nature is the least of my worries. Plus, I'm ecstatic that we're not locked in. The river of sweat pouring from my armpits subsides.

Our walk back to the boat is quiet. Completely normal for Tsvika but not for PJ. This is his dream come true, and now it's in limbo-land. It kills me to see him sad.

"PJ, you know what? Remember a few weeks ago, when you said you were going to review the municipal permits, to kick off the application process? To expedite water and electricity?

"Yeah?"

"Well, I think that's a really good idea. We have another week. May as well spend it doing due diligence, right? Plus, it may save us some time. You know how stuff moves around here."

"It's a good call, mate! Let's give her a look tomorrow!" Half of the wind returns to his sails.

We head back home and see Shawna reclined in a deck chair. True to form, she's on magazine number four of six.

"Hi! That was quick!"

"Yeah, the bank hasn't finished the docs. Another week. Island-time…"

"Well, that's good, right? It's only a week, and it gives you guys a little breathing room?"

Thank god PJ's already inside. It's not lost on me that Shawna also sees this hiatus as a positive outcome. I want to tell her that this is all a front for some bizarre anti-crime operation.

But I don't. I can't.

"Stay here. I'll come join you. Let me just check in on the computer."

"OK, but I might come inside in a few minutes. It looks like rain." I give her a long kiss.

I head to my room and fire up the computer. A note from TR has the worst subject line ever. It's only second to: *I'm late,* from a woman you slept with five weeks ago.

From: Rogers, Timothy

To: Georgeous

Subject: Good news/bad news

George—

Bad news first—Dan is not renewing his contract. His new TV show has taken off, and he doesn't have the bandwidth. He'll be transitioning out over the next two months.

Good news—The reader comments on your little quiz/advice blurbs have been excellent. David proposed that we expand the concept into something larger and that we offer you the position. You'd be running @AskEsquire—our new Twitter presence about love and relationships. Similar to Dan, you'd be sifting through Tweets and responding. The best content might even get published in the magazine. You should take this as a huge compliment. David rarely hand picks, and the fact that he referred to one of your pieces as "poignant" means that you should consider this seriously.

This is a full-time, salaried position. As a Staff Writer, you'd need to live in the States. West Coast is fine, but plan on being in New York at least twice a year.

Just to be clear, living remotely is not an option.

Congratulations on the offer. Please do get back to me with your decision as soon as possible.

Regards,

TR

When it rains it pours.

"David" is David Granger, Editor-in-Chief of Esquire. The guy is a god in New York. It could be 9pm on a Saturday night, in the newest, hottest restaurant in Manhattan, and they find the guy a table. "Right this way, Mr. Granger."

Shawna walks in. I close TR's email before you can say *poignant*.

"Everything cool with work?"

"Yeah, it's just a day of delays I guess. They're not done with the piece yet. I can do it tomorrow, after you leave. Sort of a blessing in disguise, since now we can hang out a bit more."

I'm getting so good at lying; it's starting to feel natural.

Almost.

"Great!"

She's pacing, like she's preparing for a big talk. This must be avoided at all costs. Some amount is inevitable, but I'm praying I can delay it until she's boarding her plane tomorrow.

I throw a diversion.

"Hey, for dinner? I thought we'd go somewhere nice? Celebrate your last night, Dr. Shawna?"

"That would be lovely. But I'm honestly craving a burger. Is that OK?"

I stand up and walk toward her.

"Sounds perfect." I start kissing her. Another diversion. "We can go to Lilli's. If you like it, you can bring a bottle of their hot sauce home with you." More kissing. Some clothing removal.

"Wait! Let me get my magazines out of the rain!"

I kiss her neck, and her magazine concern disappears.

•

At Lilli's, we can pull up straight to their little dock in the Minnow. Bocas version of valet. Their service? You'd need a new word for slow. But marketing is not beyond them. They've branded their own hot sauce, and all of their waitresses are thick, curvy Caribbean females that call you *papi* or *mi amor* when they take your order. I'm a sucker for it. And when you order a beer at 10am? They don't judge.

We have a few drinks. Shawna is on the mound. She winds up to throw a fastball.

"Do you ever think about reapplying to UCLA?"

"Do they have you doing recruiting now, too?"

"I thought you had your heart set on getting a Master's in Journalism?"

She's right. I spent three times the effort on my application essay as she did on hers. She got in. I didn't. The application advisor told me that my application wasn't *well-rounded enough*.

Fuck you.

But not really, as that's what really pushed me to come here and take a break. I knew the half-baked non-profit thing wouldn't hurt my chances, if I ever reapplied. And living by the water and hanging out with the kiddies is about as good as it gets. But Shawna's not wrong. My backup plan has become *the* plan.

"I didn't get in."

"I said RE-apply!"

"I was fucking summa cum laude! They're gonna take me now? Hey, I've just been getting wasted with my bro, and I've taught a few dozen kids to swim. Also, I crush it at bartending. When do I start?"

"Don't be flippant. Your story is solid. At least consider it?"

"Shawna. I'm already almost irrelevant. Quality content is dwarfed by the proliferation of social media. Facebook, Instagram, Snapchat? I could never keep up! If it weren't for PJ sending out the fucking Tweets, we'd never have any funding."

"George. You packed five t-shirts and three GRE books to come here. I was there. You can't tell me that you've given up on writing. At least not entirely, right?" She would rip my head off if she saw TR's email.

"I'm not retaking the GRE."

Our food comes. Thank god. We ordered an hour ago. We eat hungrily in silence. Their sauce is legit. Shawna finishes a big bite, and she's back on the mound.

"This is not your life! This is not REAL life! Why do you think I didn't want to go today! I am NOT supportive of this. I didn't buy you a Speedo with the Panamanian flag." I know this is only going to get worse; I may as well enjoy it.

"Oh, I thought it was just a gift, with no subtext?"

"You love punishing yourself! You do everything the hard way!"

"You told me you loved that."

Using her words against her is a cheap shot, but I can only use the tools that I have available. Otherwise, she'll bulldoze right over me.

It works.

She softens.

"I do. I do." She means it. But she's not done. "So, your writing?

You're just gonna give up and try to build a place in the jungle? I've never even seen you even hold a hammer!"

"Shawna. I know you are coming from a place of love. I don't want to fight you. I am trying to build a life here. Trying to do something. Can you just try to be supportive?" Cheap shot #2. I'm referencing one of her diatribes from a few days ago, and she knows it.

"I am supportive. And I do love you. I just want you to come home." Hard to argue with that. She kisses me on the cheek. "This last week has been incredible. Do what you want. I know I said I don't want to get back together, but I lied. I want you to come home. Come home to me."

Ugh.

I'm pissed that I actually find her offer tempting. I pull out my secret weapon—silence.

I wait.

We wait.

To show her that I'm not dismissing this, I order us two more drinks. It's completely false, because I want to get up and walk right out of the restaurant. But sometimes pretending to be committed helps you get there. I can't wait any longer.

"Shawna. I did anything and everything for you. I loved you the best I possibly could. And you cheated on me. For what?"

She's been waiting for this, and I can see, by the look on her face, that her answer is prepared.

"You showed me your love by doing things. But you never understood that I didn't want you to spend ten hours helping me with my admissions essay. What I wanted was for you to spend ten seconds telling me that you needed me. That you loved me and couldn't live without me."

"You couldn't have just said that? You had to fuck some guy to say it?"

"Do I regret it? Yes. Every day. Every single day. Am I sorry? I've never been more sorry in my life. There's nothing I regret more. But do you want to know what hurts even worse?"

No, I don't. Not really.

I focus on my food. I will the one tear in my eye not to fall. And I especially will myself to stay silent.

"You came here. You may have run away, but it's changed you. You're both more peaceful and more intense. You treat me how I want to be treated, even if only for a week. And the thing is, it's not because of me. You didn't change for me. You changed for you. Bocas changed you. I'm so fucking jealous of this place; I can't stand it."

Goddamn, she is insightful and incisive.

"Do you still talk to him?" She sees this coming, too.

"I did. And then he finally had to tell me that he got his TA pregnant."

"What?"

"Yeah. Karma's a bitch, eh? She's due in three months."

"Wow. I can't tell if I'm glad or mad or jealous or all three."

"I couldn't care less. He's just a bump on a road that I'll never cross again."

Her resolution makes me feel better. A little. But just hearing about his life makes the hot sauce in my stomach growl.

"George. I broke my promise. I fell for you. Again. And I'm frustrated that now that I'm ready to accept you for who you are, you don't want it." Her eyes well up. "I want to be with you. I want to try. And if you don't, that's OK. It would crush me, but I already know that I've lost you. I am so, so sorry. I hope you know that."

She starts crying so hard—I can't help but kiss her on the forehead. She kisses my cheek and cries. I rock her back and forth. The pendulous movement makes my eyes wander. And land on…Primo.

Jesus Christ.

The fucker is drinking an Orange Fanta. And he's chatting with one of the voluptuous wait-staff. There's something satisfying about a 250lb man drinking a dainty fruit drink. I hope he asks for a straw.

Please, please tell me that it's just a coincidence that he's here.

The waitress slides a straw over.

Victory.

He looks at me and nods, to tell me that he knows that I'm here. Or, so that I know that he's here.

Shawna is almost done, but she's still a mess. Our waitress looks over at us, nonplussed. She's seen it all before. Those gringos love to cry. Shawna leaves tomorrow. In some ways, I wish she could become a bump in the road that I'll never cross again. But the way I'm hugging her tells me that's far from being true.

We finish our meal and return to the previous days' rhythm. No more talking.

Primo leaves.

But only after giving me the eye one more time.

We pay. I set tender Shawna in the Minnow.

Dealing with her and my clandestine other life is just too much.

9

How to understand the constant female subtext:

When your girl says you make her feel safe, it's not because you can protect her from fifteen MS 13 gang members with face tattoos. It's because when she's with you, she's not alone.

I can't sleep. I hit the power on the computer. Shawna doesn't even stir. I have to reread TR's email one more time, just to make sure it's real.

It is.

I give in and write my mom.

From: Georgeous
To: Ms. Lewis

Subject: from your long lost son

hi mom—

just a little check-in email. things are going great here. shawna came for

a little bit and leaves tomorrow. super fun. i know the flight is long, but

you should think about coming.

miss you, love you.

george

I know there's no content in that email, but it's all I can muster.

She does not need to know about me going to Colombia, automatic

weapons trafficking or ludicrous real estate investments. In due time.

Shawna turns toward me.

"Hey."

"Hey, sleepyface."

"What are you doing?"

"Writing my mom."

"Really?"

Even I'm surprised that it's not a lie.

"Yeah. Just a few lines. It'd been a while."

"Come to bed." I put the computer to sleep and crawl in.

Her body is warm. I wish it still felt like home, but it doesn't. Not

after our last talk. It feels more like a nice hotel—one that you enjoy

but also look forward to checking out of. Just leave the key card on the

dresser.

We start kissing. And grabbing.

She's rougher. Biting me. Her nails drag across my back, and I can feel that they're leaving marks. I respond similarly, more forcefully. I push into her. Deep. Hard. I don't know where this side of us came from.

Maybe I do.

My sweat drops onto her stomach, and she can feel me swell…

"Come inside me…please. Please, come inside me."

I do.

And now she has my seed.

I roll over, wishing I could take it back.

•

Shawna's on the 7:30am flight back to Panama City. It's balls early, but the only other option is flying into the smaller regional airport and cabbing to PTY. Panama's not as dangerous as some of the other countries in Central America, but the risk of becoming an express-hostage still exists. For solo gringo travelers it could go one of two ways—either you have a pleasant conversation in broken Spanish with a cabbie, or you end up shoeless and penniless in an ATM vestibule. If you're a woman? They take a lot more than your purse.

"Do you need any snacks for the plane? I brought Peanut M&Ms and those fried plantains you liked."

"You're the best. Let's open the M&Ms right now."

"Done."

The emotions and marathon bone session from last night have left us clingy. She leans against me in the security line, and I can feel the neck of my t-shirt wet with her tears. I pull her in. A cockroach scurries across the linoleum. Maybe three inches long? Must be a baby. No need to alert Shawna.

She's next up in line.

"Bye, sweetie."

"Keep writing me, OK?"

"Do I have to iMessage? It's weird."

"Just whatever. Email is fine. Bye. I love you."

"I love you, too."

There's only one gate, so I keep my eyes on her for a few minutes. They board right away.

•

PJ hears me coming in the Minnow and runs out to the dock. He's holding a brand new surfboard.

"G'day, mate!"

"When did you get that? It looks perfect!"

"Yestahday. She's a beauty, ay?" He holds it up for us both to admire. All of the fins even match. "I got the guy from Tropix to have it shipped ovah from my mate in Costa Rica. He's got a little shaping shop in Povones." He admires it again. "Mates rates, 'course! Fancy a dip?"

"No, go ahead. I'm beat. You should have enough gas to get you to Ponch, but get some on your way back. Do you need cash? I have some."

"Nah, sorted."

"Cool. I'm going back to bed. Maybe watch a flick on your laptop a little later on?"

"Absolutely. Check yah bed. Little pressie for yah."

"Ha. OK. Have fun."

He speeds off in the Minnow. Hellman.

In my room, I look at my bed. He's laid out a t-shirt on my pillow: *I Kind of Think Your Triangle is Being Obtuse.*

It's puzzling, but I like it.

I try it on in front of the bathroom mirror, and there's a Post-It from Tsvika:

G—

Let's move the boxes this week.

T

Translation: the guns are getting moved this week. I'd like to think that he's telling me to be careful, but he isn't. He's telling me to be alert. So I can be his backup plan.

Fuck him.

•

I just want this day to end. I do all of my laundry, attempt to nap, fail and clean the kitchen into oblivion.

I'm so fragile, I agree to watch *Priscilla Queen of the Desert* with PJ. His raucous laughter soothes me, and I pass out on the floor of his room.

•

In the morning, I walk into the kitchen, wearing the shirt.

"Fits nice, ay!"

"PJ, it's perfect. Geometry puns. I love it."

"To be honest, I don't really get it. But you're such a numbah crunchah! And I've heard you call The Praúler obtuse a few times."

"Have I?"

"All the time."

"I love it. Thank you. I'm going to take it off right now so I don't sweat through it before work. Lady patrons of the Barco Hundido? You're welcome."

"Nice one. What time you headin' in?"

"Two or so? We need to do inventory."

"Perfect! Hop in with yah? I wanna hit up the municipality and then do some measurements at the property. Thirsty for a bottle of piss 'round six?"

"Sure, but let's hook up for a drink after I get off work? Raúl is all over The Wreck these days."

"Suitcha self. I'll see what's crackin' at Mondo."

"Cool. And if we pull this thing off, can we get a bigger boat? Running a business with the Minnow would be ridiculous. Think about it. Snorkeling tours are not even an option." PJ lights up with excitement.

"I like where yah head's at!"

I pour us the last of the coffee.

"Alright. I'm gonna do some work. See you in a bit."

You know how when you lie enough, you start to believe the lie yourself? That's where my head is with the Surf & Shag Shack. I can actually picture our lives there, even though it's felt doomed from the get-go. Hopefully our fictitious future boat has an electric starter.

I need to respond to TR; it's been almost two days. Shawna has made it home. And, of course, she's written.

From: Shawna B.

To: Georgeous

Subject: Aye Papi!

Is that how they say it? Anyway, I'm home safe. A couple of days with my mom and then back to reality. She bought a color printer at Costco, and she is (don't get mad) making a scrapbook of my trip. She's asked me three hundred questions about the starfish. You are so glad you're not here.

Anyway, I just wanted to check in.

I had such a wonderful time. Thank you.

Xxiiiiiiiiiioo (Is that how many boners you had? Couldn't keep track.)

Shawna

PS If you iMessage me, I'll have sext with you. Maybe even FaceTime, if you SWEAR no screenshots.

Shawna knows what she's doing. She said that she wanted to be with me while she was here. I didn't respond. Now she's changing tactics—trying to reach my heart through my dick.

It's not the worst approach.

Still procrastinating, I can't keep myself from responding to Shawna before writing back to TR.

From: Georgeous

To: Shawna B.

Subject: aye, mamita!

yes, that's how you say it. so hot, you speaking spanish.

i had so much fun with you, too.

and by that, I mean the aggressive sex we have after the big talks you live for.

it's charming that your mom loves starfish.

does she want one?

there's one living atop a discarded can of red bull in our bay. i'll ask marquito to keep it gently preserved.

g

ps i abhor our generation's lack of sense of community, and therefore, need to constantly be in touch through these false environments—aka social media and instant messaging. wait, didju say i get to see your tits? i'm in.

Our email feels intimate, but I also can't wait for the day when Shawna is so absent from my thoughts that I have to remind myself to think about her.

•

My set of keys for The Wreck is pretty limited; I can only do so much. And there's not a chance that I'm stepping foot into the dry storage room. I walk around, check all of the lights, pick up random pieces of trash and grab the rogue floaters on the fringes. A handful of beer cans have slipped in, near the sunken ship itself.

Besides Primo as head Henchman, there is a slightly smaller (but still massive) version of him that now works full-time security at The Wreck. I have no idea what his name is. His temperament has two dimensions: complete silence or the occasional laugh—at me being a gringo. I have nicknamed him: Mr. Personality.

I've done all of the tinkering I can do. I burn an hour flipping through some ancient surf magazines. Mr. P looks as bored babysitting me as I am being babysat.

Since the episode with Andrea's necklace, Raúl has been letting me hop into the water around The Wreck and to do little cleanups. I love it. I drop in, and Mr. P waits as I pass him up a few cans. I swim around The Wreck and see a bottle lodged way underneath. I grab it. Ouch! The back of my hand gets snagged by a reefy outcrop. I pop to the surface.

"Fuck!"

Mr. P sees me babying my hand.

"Hay sangre?" And the blood starts pouring out. He laughs. "Con cuidado." Be careful? Dick. I've got the ladder with one hand, but he still pulls me out. Thank god we have hydrogen peroxide somewhere. I always keep waterproof Band-Aids handy, in case I get cut at work.

It's not too bad. I clean it, put a bandage on it and get back in.

What else am I going to do?

The sunlight catches a faded can of Panama, nestled in the sand. It's the beer they use for beer bongs at Mondo Taitu. I grab it.

What the fuck am I doing here?

I should have instantly accepted TR's offer and gotten on the next plane out of here, bringing PJ with me. I visualize PJ and I crashing at

Shawna's, and I'm annoyed with myself at how easily I default to her.

Picturing PJ giggling on Shawna's couch in LA makes me smile. Then a wave of guilt hits me. I've got to tell him about Tsvika. I'll do it tonight. And then I'll accept TR's offer and book a flight home next week.

But for now? It's business as usual. My number one priority is making sure Raúl only thinks of me as George—his obedient gringo employee.

It's bizarre to have a moment of clarity, while holding a piece of trash. Mr. P throws it into the recycling bin, but I know that it will eventually get mixed together with the regular trash, on the way to the dump.

Just having a plan calms me. I am going to be a Staff Writer. That's pretty damn cool. Poignant, even.

•

A long boring night at The Wreck and I'm dead on my feet. Swimming home, I drag my heels in the sand in front of our house, delaying confronting PJ. It's funny, the thought of telling Tsvika that I'm ejecting hasn't even crossed my mind, and he's undoubtedly the first person I should tell.

But the house is completely empty.

Odd.

There's a note on the kitchen counter:

Georgie—

Met a few birds and heading over to Aqua. Join us? The brunette's a tall one—all yours, mate!

PJ

Procrastination.

There's only one thing I can do, and it's the easiest task of all—saying yes to TR. Out of habit, I re-proofread my latest assignment.

From: Georgeous

To: Rogers, Timothy

Subject: RE: Good news/bad news

Attachment: EsquisiteSavage17_GL_clean.doc

TR—

My recent revisions are attached. They were quite light this time. I just attached the clean file.

Regarding your offer: first, I am immeasurably flattered that Mr. Granger has read my work at all. That is a personal triumph.

I need to wrap up a few things here, but I should be able to do that in the next month or two, during Dan's transition period.

Therefore, I graciously accept the offer!

Again, I am sincerely humbled and appreciative, especially of you, Tim, for looking out for me. I know we've never been super close, but I am very thankful to have you in my corner. As a colleague and a friend.

I hope that all made sense.

Sincerely,

George

Goddamn, what a sense of relief. I fall into bed, fantasize about the adult work clothes I'll have to buy from Nordstrom Rack and doze.

•

PJ has already eaten, and I'm not hungry, so we head out. Thank god, because I did not want to have the conversation, *PJ, what are you hungry for? How about a steaming plateful of lies?* And there's no way I can tell him what's been going on right now, as we head straight toward The Wreck. PJ wears his heart on his sleeve, and Raúl will sense it on him, like a shark smelling blood in the water.

I have to talk to him tonight. This secret keeping is eating me alive.

We get about a quarter of the way to The Wreck, and I can't help but whistle the theme song to *Gilligan's Island*. I look at PJ. He smiles and whistles along with me for a few bars. Then I cast us:

PJ—Gilligan. But Gilligan after P90X.

Raúl—The Skipper. Because he's always pissed at Gilligan.

The Millionaire (Thurston Howell III)—Tsvika. No brainer, due to his palatial pad and never really working.

His Wife (Mrs. Howell)—Andrea. Since she came to the tropics with a boyfriend (albeit leaving him back home).

The Movie Star— Vanesa. A seductress but asks you to, *lock the door on the way out, Papi.* Heartbreaker.

The Professor—Me. It's ambitious, but it's probably the closest.

Mary Ann—Shawna. Slam dunk.

We tie up, and I whistle the chorus:

If not for the courage of the fearless crew,
The Minnow would be lost.

The Minnow would be lost.

Hmmm. I'm not sure if I have Raúl cast accurately as the Skipper.

The Wreck is completely empty. Bizarre. Raúl never leaves without at least one of his gorillas here.

"Weird, huh?"

"Yeah, kinda creepy, ay?"

"God, I hope he comes back with a posse. I'm not sure my back can handle a full restock by myself. Eighty cases? Jesus."

"Maybe I can help when I'm back, mate?"

"Good idea. You do need to work off your tab, but just not tonight, OK? Raul's on a tear these days."

"OK."

"Promise me, PJ."

"I promise! Don't get so hectic!"

I think PJ is going to finally call me out, for being aloof. But he doesn't.

"Sorry, I just…"

"Georgie, no worries. It is yah job, ay?" PJ and I sometimes compete for number one pleaser. "Iguana's got a new bartendah. Just broke up with her bloke…"

"Can't wait to meet her at breakfast."

PJ laughs and drops a coy smile.

"Aw mate! I didn't tell you! The city has plans to PAVE our road! All the way to The Bluffs! We'll be millionaires!"

"Very cool." My excitement is hollow, but it doesn't bother him.

"Alright, catch yas in a bit. Hopefully the person running the

permit office today is a bird!" He drops his magic smile. May god have
mercy on her.

An hour passes. The Praúler, Primo and a few others show up.

"Flacito."

"Buenas. El inventorio hoy, no?" I want him to know that I've
been here, waiting to do the inventory. Business as usual.

"Nosotros tenemos." We've got it. Oh, right. No white dudes in
the secret room.

"Bueno. El barco? Tan latas." We both look down at the water,
spotting two decaying cans of Balboa resting on the bottom. Even after
yesterday, it can still use a cleanup.

"Sí, si quieres." If you want. Now I see where Marquito gets his
language skills. I grab my goggles and put trunks on. Shawna's
flashlight has been perfect for this task.

I pop in the water and swim around, slowly. I grab a bottle deep
underneath. When I pull it out with my hand, I can't believe yesterday's
Band-Aid is still intact.

I go a little further under the deck and hit the flashlight. Complete
wasteland. Since the bar extends way out over the water, the planks on
the inland side—closest to the entrance—start right after a short, three-
foot beach. Trapped underneath those initial planks are hundreds of
cans, bottles and cigarette butts, because it's so shallow.

Disgusting.

It's gotta wait for another day. Who knows what else is living in the
miniature bay of trash. I grab some air in a little pocket, underneath the
main bar, and spot two more Balboa cans. I can't wait to be home

tonight, sipping on a few myself with PJ.

"Georgie?"

Speak of the devil.

"I'm down here. Look below deck."

"Ah, gettin' a dip in, ay?"

"What are you doing here? I told you…"

"I know, mate! But I was getting cornahed!"

"By who?"

"Remember that bird? At the bank?"

"The loan officer you shagged?"

"Made love to, mate, please…anyway, her hubbie's on the hunt fah me!"

"William Hurt, in the Tommy Bahamas shirt?" I chuckle at my own rhyme.

"Ay? It's not funny. He's been lookin' all ovah town fah me! Guess I left a shirt under the mattress!"

"*Mozzarella Stick Vegetarian?*"

"Yeah! How'd you know?"

"Lucky guess. But dude, get OUT of here. If Raúl sees you, he's going to kill you. And me."

"A'right a'right, keep yah pants on. Just wanted to snag the keys to the Minnow."

"For sure. They're in my shorts, over on that empty crate."

"Cheers."

To kill time until I hear the Minnow's motor start and PJ gone, I take my goggles off, clean them with some spit and put them back on.

I catch a glimpse of PJ, heading toward the dry storage.

Nooo.

He's helped me stock a million times before. It's second nature for him to grab a case on his way across the bar, to help me out, before he takes off.

Fuck. Fuck. Fuck.

He is a thoughtful creature of habit.

"AYE! NO PASAS!"

"Ay? I'm just helping Georgie! Relax!" Uh oh. I swim back toward the ladder. Ouch! Half of the Band-Aid rips off, as I grab the bottom rung.

PJ is carrying a case of Balboa, walking backwards, away from Primo. Primo is pointing a 9mm at him.

Jesus Christ.

I climb out of the water. Reflexively, I put my hands up, even though I really want to take my goggles off. Primo scowls at the flashlight in my hand, and then he aims the gun at me. Raúl barks at him.

"NO."

Primo points the gun back at PJ.

"Todo bien…todo bien. Tranquilo, Primo." I try to defuse. PJ keeps backing away from Primo, until he's directly in front of me.

"WOOOGHF." What? We all stop and look. La Policia Nacional are flying straight at us, in a gunship.

BOOM. BOOM. BOOM. Three warning shots are fired into the air, from a fifty caliber mounted on the front of the cruiser. It's deafening.

Primo's eyes widen. You guys did this.

BAM. He shoots PJ. The force of the shot slams PJ back into me, and we fly off the back of the deck.

PJ and I careen to the bottom, in a forced spoon position. The weight of the case of beer on his chest drives us down, and the pressure of the quick decent feels like it's going to rupture my eardrums.

SLAM.

We hit the bottom. His body slams into my ribs. I gasp, letting out half of my air.

Fuck.

BOOM. BOOM. BOOM. It sounds like a dogfight in Kabul up there. PJ's blood clouds the water. We were on top of the deck ten seconds ago, but it feels like we've been down here an hour. PJ is moving, but barely, and I see the last of his air escape.

I wiggle out from underneath him, keeping the case of beer on him as an anchor. Goddamn, my ribs hurt. But my goggles are still intact— miracle. I tap his chest three times, to let him know what's coming. He starts to writhe. I grab the back of his head and give him a tiny bit of air. We only have one shot, and I know if I give it to him all at once, the unexpected burst will overwhelm him.

He gasps. I wait two seconds. I tap his chest three times again. Gun shell casings slowly sink down and settle in the sand, and the police cruiser has moved right above us.

Pulling PJ into a full-blown make out, I slowly give him all the air I've got. He sucks it in.

It's time.

I slide the case of beer off of him. It weighs four tons underwater. He's still mostly limp, but his survival skills are intact. When I slap his hand against my leg, he grips it. Damn, he is strong. Up we go.

My flashlight catches the propeller from the idling cruiser. Backing up is not an option.

I change course. I head us to the far end of the deck, where I know we'll be covered. And there's air.

I suck in air like my life depends on it. Because it fucking does. I yank my leg up and grab PJ's hand. He comes up and coughs. I have to hold him up. The little Band-Aid hanging off my hand looks ridiculous. Letting PJ rest on my shoulder, I adjust my grip on the flashlight. Without it, we would have been shot by now.

"WOOOGHF WOOOGHF WOOOGHF." Wiglaf has jumped onto the deck and is hauling ass somewhere. Why is Wiglaf here and not on a leash?

Primo and posse must have broken into the stash, because the gunfire triples. PJ coughs from the smoke. I can see combat boots right above us. The wood splinters, a bullet grazes my hand and Mr. Combat Boots takes some hits. Please let him be wearing a bulletproof vest.

The bullet's path against my skin has replaced the Band-Aid with gushing blood.

True irony.

Our little fort is not safe.

I tap PJ's chest again, three times. Hard.

Like Pavlov, he sucks in his own air. One of us has to anchor us, otherwise we'll float back to the top. PJ is way more buoyant than Marquito playing Jortuga. I exhale every ounce of my air. I would be pissed, but I still have the flashlight, and my goggles remain intact. I'm feeling pretty lucky.

I'm thinking the center bar's density is our best bet. The buoyancy of PJ's air keeps yanking us up, so I have to pull us there, foot-by-foot, gripping onto the sunken ship. With every grab, the crustaceans shred my hand. It feels like putting on a baseball mitt, filled with broken glass.

We make it and both gasp.

What is gunpowder, potassium nitrate? Whatever it is, the air filled with it tastes fantastic, compared to drowning.

PJ is barely breathing. His eyes flutter. The water must be draining all the blood out of his body. We can't stay. Three more chest taps, and he takes in a little dribble of air.

The remainder of the bar is on stilts. I grab them and pull us along quickly. All of them are covered in barnacles and sharp living creatures. My left hand feels like it went through a paper shredder. With all of the potential nerve damage, I wonder if I will ever type again. At least I'll always be able to hold a flashlight, with my right.

We surface.

The gunshots cease. I drag PJ out of the water and onto the filthy little beach. A ton of shouting. Two more gunshots. I apply pressure to his wound, and it wakes him. He smiles.

"Always knew you were a poof, mate…"

"Hang on! I've got you!"

I look up at fifteen dudes in fatigues.

"AYUDA!" HELP! One of them raises his gun at me. But someone pushes his hand down. PJ reaches out to me, but he's so weak, he just grazes my arm.

"Waste of a crate of Balbies, aaayyy...?"

His head falls back. Team camo pulls us out. They lay PJ out, and one of them goes to work. I'm pretty impressed with the Panamanian government's medical training.

Bodies are lying everywhere, either handcuffed or surrounded by blood. I catch a glimpse of Tsvika, in a bulletproof vest, talking to what looks like the head honcho of La Policia Nacional. Tsvika looks me in the eyes and then at my body. He turns to the head honcho, pointing. Not at PJ. At me.

I follow his gaze and look down at myself. I'm covered in blood, both PJ's and mine. I can see the trajectory of the bullet across my hand and wrist. So sleepy. My head drops, and the last thing I see is the tiny, littered beer-can beach—soaked in blood.

Blackness.

10

How sensitive you should be:

> *Be able to pick out a nice bottle of Pinot Noir for a dinner party, but never hesitate to break it over some motherfucker's head if he disrespects your lady.*

BEEP. BEEP. BEEP. BEEP. What is that annoying sound? Oh, my heart on the monitor.

So thirsty.

"Enfermera? Enfermera?" Nurse?

My throat is killing me.

A woman with a stethoscope walks in.

"Señor Lewis, todo bien?"

My voice sounds like the Marlboro Man, and I feel like I swam in a bathtub of Abuelo.

"Tengo sed." I'm thirsty.

"Por su puesto. Un momento." I can hear her talking, but it's distant.

The doc returns. She makes two clicking sounds near my head, and my jaw starts to feel creamy.

I hear them talking in the hallway.

"Señor Lewis…"

A crew of technicians comes in, and they go to work.

Pain.

That tube they pull out of your nose does not feel bueno. I close my eyes. They treat my body like an old Honda at Jiffy Lube. When they pull the restraints from my wrists, I look at my watch. Someone took it off and switched it to my right wrist. Thoughtful.

Two days.

Whoa.

I fall back asleep.

●

Time passes. An hour. A day. I have no idea. Like an airplane penetrating the clouds, I begin to fully wake up. More pain. Headache. They leave the IV in my arm. The tannest male doctor on earth walks in. A gringo.

"Mr. Lewis. How are you feeling?"

"Where's the…" the gravel in my voice slows me. But he's heard this question before.

"Dr. Esperanza is our chief of surgery and my boss. I'm your attending physician."

He looks me over.

"You went to med school, in the States, Canada?"

His stethoscope is freezing.

"University of Michigan. Grew up in Pennsylvania. Came here for residency, never went back." The story I've heard a hundred times. It's fucking Bocas. "You will be fine, but you have severely bruised ribs and countless contusions. We've kept you on a steady drip of antibiotics to avoid infection. It took a team hours to stitch up your left hand."

"I can feel it."

"I'm sure. We'll keep your pain meds up, but we need to get you home, to heal. The bacteria that breed in hospitals are extremely dangerous to someone with your number of lacerations." The hospital full of bacteria reminds me of the ATM without money. "One of the nurses has volunteered to stay with you, for the first few days. You've got quite a fan club here."

"Not Dr. Esperanza?" He smiles. It's probably his wife.

"Unfortunately for you, no." He breaks with a smile. "A male nurse will attend to you." I hear PJ calling me a poof.

PJ!

"Doctor! PJ? Where is he?" His eyes find the floor.

"His trauma was severe. He died in transit. I am so sorry."

I stare at him. Tears come fast. He reaches out and pats my leg.

"You need to get some rest now."

He reaches next to my head. *Click-click.*

I picture drinking Balboas underwater with PJ and realize that the drugs just hit. Sneaky tan fucker.

•

Twelve hours disappear. I feel like I drank a gallon of chirrisco, the
Panamanian moonshine they distill in the hills. They accelerate the
fermentation by adding battery acid. No joke.

My eyes crack open.

Tsvika is sitting across from me.

"Stop blowing spit bubbles." His saliva is so viscous. Disgusting.

"George. You are feeling OK?"

"What the fuck, Tsvika? PJ is dead? Dead?"

"Yes."

"And that couldn't be avoided?"

"No. I am sorry."

If I could stand, I'd choke him.

Tsvika nods toward a nurse. She approaches my IV. I'd never
thought of doctors and nurses as bartenders before. But damn, if they
don't get you fucked up.

"GET THE FUCK OUT OF HERE."

It's like he was waiting for me to say it. He stands. Before I see him
walk out, my eyes close.

•

The male nurse, Manuelo, has become my friend, confidante and
bodyguard. He's the only one I tell the entire story to, in broken
Spanish. Word of me being in the hospital spreads, and every single
person I've ever served a beer to in Bocas tries to come visit. But an
Israeli dude stands at the front of my door to my hospital room,
around the clock. It's complete overkill, but I appreciate the privacy.

For days, I lack for nothing in the hospital. But all I want is to get out of here. They change my dressings three times a day. My left hand and wrist have over a hundred stitches. Manuelo wheels me out.

I ask for my bill. $0.

Dr. Esperanza has been checking on me, too. She gives me a kiss on the cheek and calls me "Un caballero." Either a gentleman or a cowboy. Can she come back to Carenero with us?

I still ache all over, dreading the boat ride.

Manuelo wheels me two blocks to an obscure dock. Tsvika's waiting for us. He's been busy and is sporting a new top-of-the-line boat. I want to comment, but I'm so happy we don't have to endure the Minnow. I muscle through the ride—much smoother in the twenty foot Panga. Apparently Israeli operatives are paid well.

Home.

Two of Tsvika's video game/actual ninja friends emerge from the house. They'd better not have been eating PJ's Los Crunchberries.

They set me in bed. It feels fantastic, but damn, it hurts. Manuelo is Johnny-on-the-spot.

"Tienes dolor?" Are you in pain?

"Sí. Mucho." He opens the Percocet bottle and offers me one. My eyes say: make it two. He does. Manuelo, you're my boy.

"Con una Balboa?"

"Media Balboa." You can have half a beer.

Manuelo is an impressive negotiator. He comes back with a frosty Balbie, and I wash them down. Three sips in, I start taking long, long blinks. He grabs the can.

PANAMANIAC!!! I'm really warming to recreational drug use.

•

Ahhh. I wake up feeling better. Looking at my watch, I've slept for fifteen hours. Manuelo has dozed, but he hears me move and jumps up.

"Todo bien?"

"Sí, hoy, más mejor." I really do feel a lot better.

"Quires cafecita?" Coffee?

"Sí, por favor, gracias. Y tambien el computador de PJ, en su alcoba? El laptop?" I'm guessing he's afraid to go in PJ's room, but the thought of sitting in the chair in front of the old iMac I bought here for $400 sounds awful. He takes off for the kitchen.

Tsvika walks in, two minutes later, carrying a new MacBook box, without the plastic wrapping.

"You need computer? The boss. Esquire. They send. I open. Confirm the power charging."

"Whoa."

He opens the box and sets it next to me. Tsvika is not one to dawdle and exits.

The computer boots in a millisecond.

Holy fuck—I have thirty emails. I scroll down to the bottom. It's TR responding to my email, over a week ago now.

From: Rogers, Timothy

To: Georgeous

Subject: RE: RE: Good news/bad news

George—

Wonderful news. Welcome aboard. Regarding "wrapping up" your life in paradise over the next few months—unfortunately, that will be difficult. You'll be working with a small team of people, and we are planning to have you here—in New York—within the next few weeks, to begin the transition.

Let's discuss. Give me a call tomorrow (or Skype is fine).

Looking forward to working together,

TR

Uh oh.

That deadline has long passed. I hit reply. Manuelo comes back in with the most epic coffee I've ever tasted. I'm glad he made one for himself, too.

"Delicioso. Mil gracias."

"Por nada, Don Jorge." He speaks to me with reverence. Shamelessly, I love being called Don Jorge. Then he goes back to reading the Spanish edition of *People Magazine*. I wouldn't mind reading it when he's done.

I stare back at my empty email response.

Not right now.

I reread his email in the preview pane, and then sort by his name. He wrote me again, a few days ago.

From: Rogers, Timothy

To: Georgeous

Subject: My deepest condolences

I am so sorry to hear about your friend.

Your roommate Svika(?) contacted us a few days ago. Forgive me for guessing at the spelling of his name, but he is quite resourceful, that one.

What little he shared of the story sounds harrowing, to say the least.

We are all thrilled to hear that you are OK. Again, I am so sorry to hear about your friend. I understand you two were quite close.

I hope it is not an imposition, but I did call the hospital to check on you.

Word is that you will have a full recovery. Wonderful news.

David also called a few folks. He retroactively changed your status to "In the field, on assignment." So, if any medical bills pop up, you are covered.

On a lighter note, my overzealous admin had your business cards printed. They are on my desk. She also had your staff computer configured and FedEx'ed to Panama. Don't worry about work. We thought it might be useful to have it bedside, while convalescing.

At some point, we should discuss your return to the States. But for now, just rest up. Take whatever time you need, and do let me know if you need anything.

I wish you a speedy recovery.

Drop me a line, when you are well.

Best,

TR

PS This may be tough to fathom right now, but do consider writing about your experience. Would make a great short feature and tribute to your friend.

    I scroll down and read a note from Shawna.

From: Shawna B.

To: Georgeous

Subject: PLEASE LET ME KNOW YOU ARE OK!!!

George! Please send me a note when you can!

I'm so so sorry about PJ. It's awful. So awful. I don't know what to

say…

You must be devastated.

I'm so sorry, George.

I got a call from Tsvika. How did he find me???

Anyway, he says you are good and that they are keeping an eye on you.

Hopefully you are healing up and everything will return to normal.

Please come home. Of course you can always stay with me.

I love you, so much. Let me know if you need anything, OK?

Shawna

PS Just to end on something nice, I know you're not a fan of

Facebook, but take a look when you have a chance. TTTS racked up

$650 in donations last week! You've made a lot of friends in Bocas!

    I send her a quick one.

From: Georgeous

To: Shawna B.

Subject: RE: PLEASE LET ME KNOW YOU ARE OK!!!

i'm fine.

hurts to type.

more later.

tell my mom I'm ok?

xo

g

I'm guessing that Tsvika had all of our communications monitored, otherwise, he'd not have been able to make contact with Shawna and TR.

I get pissed, thinking about some computer geek in Israel reading Shawna and my racy email exchanges. But I also notice that he didn't notify my mother. For that, I am grateful.

Creepy wiretapping motherfucker.

I close the laptop and cry. And cry. And cry. Manuelo takes his *People en Español* to the kitchen. He's left my meds next to me, and I pop a Perco. Ten minutes later, I can hear PJ yelling at Mel Gibson in *Gallipoli*.

"Don't do it, Gibso!"

No wonder people love drugs so much.

But maybe not so much. Because seeing him makes me miss him. And really wish I wasn't one of the characters in the background of *Gallipoli* that lived.

After a nap, it's time to get out of bed. Other than rubbing the bar of soap against my ribs, the shower feels amazing. The cuts are healing well. Coming out in my towel, I see that Manuelo is studying *Who Wore it Best?* After all the drama, it's nice to see someone doing something so simple and mindless. We talk briefly about how obvious the answer is—Rashida Jones' flawless skin really makes the couture dress pop.

"Manuelo. Muchismas gracias por todo. Estoy curado. Ir a casa, por favor." I'm all better. It's time for you to go home, brother.

"Pero no! No está curado!" No, you are not!

But I'm cured enough. I tuck the towel at my waist and reach into the reserve cash stash in my desk. I find a pristine hundred-dollar bill.

"Un regalito."

His eyes pop.

"No. Absolutamente, no." I tuck it into his shirt pocket. He's so handsome—I'm thankful I'm straight. Because I could never pull him—he's way out of my league.

"Absolutamente, sí. Un abrazito." He gives me a light hug, careful of the ribs. What an amazing guy.

Sanity has restored to the house. The Israeli dudes have left. Only Tsvika remains.

On a late morning, I pop a beer can open with a spoon.

Ouch.

My left hand is still tender.

Tsvika walks in.

"Tsviks. Can you do me a favor?"

"Yes. Of course."

Tsvika should consider a second career as a personal assistant.

"Find Marco."

Poor Marquito. Both parents dead. Even if Raúl could have withstood the five gunshot wounds, he didn't stand a chance against Wiglaf's mauling. Wiglaf ripped Raúl's body to shreds, before Primo's crew emptied a full clip into him. Damn, I even miss Wiglaf.

Why Raúl kept Primo from shooting me, I will never know. It does confirm that he didn't find the GPS or even suspect it. I'll also never know if Raúl had Primo keeping an eye on me, or if I was just being paranoid. Raúl saved me. And I betrayed him. And I betrayed PJ, with this stupid undercover game.

The tears return.

I have reverse-engineered the scenario a thousand times, trying to find a version where PJ doesn't get shot. But I never find one. I search and search and then eventually return to the same place.

"Marco is fine. He stay with grandmother of Primo."

"Would you mind getting him and bringing him here?"

"No problem."

"Tsviks?"

"Yes?"

"Why?" Silence. And a stare. "It just doesn't make sense. Can you tell me anything? So much effort to go after a small-time criminal. And with PJ…"

"George. Raúl was bad guy. Many things you do not know. Not more to say."

I always knew that the search for clarity, in life, is hopeless. But this takes the cake. To have the biggest event in my life occur and not know why haunts me.

"Should I have told you that I'd be there early for inventory? I can't let it go. Fucking PJ, I tried…"

Tsvika softens in such a tiny way; you'd never see it if you weren't his roommate.

"George. Criminals? We cannot control. Where weapons go? We try to control."

I can't argue with that.

It kills me that PJ was collateral damage.

But I get it.

Nothing can be undone.

I throw him a bone.

"PJ is…ehhh…was… a force that could not be controlled."

"Yes. Strong energy he has."

"Strong energy. Agreed. It's too bad about the land."

"The land? No, no. We buy."

"Huh?"

"My family. We already buy. We give share to PJ family."

"Really?"

"My family. Real estate business. Is small token."

I don't fully believe him, but it doesn't matter.

"But Tsvika, I can't do it."

"No, no. My father, he pay. Already. How do you say? Is not much money."

"Seventy-five grand. He could just write a check for it." Maybe his father is also a spy? *My Mossad Dad* would make a great movie title.

"Correct."

"What about the loan?"

It's the first time I've seen him almost smile. Almost.

"PJ was boss, of hotel. Yes. But loan? Don't need." I take it all in for a minute. The Tsviks is not one to fill dead air with words.

"Indeed. PJ was the boss. So who's gonna run the Surf and Shag Shack?"

"Everything the same. We build hotel."

"Tsvika! I'm out! It's not happening! Why would I stay?"

"No, no. Not now. We build the places. The house. The bungalows. It take one year. Maybe more. If you want, come back. You can be Manager. No problem. Teach the swimming. But now, George, you must leave Bocas. Not safe for you here."

•

I see Marquito the next day. He's shell-shocked, so basically the same as he was before. We talk. OK. I talk.

It's time to go home.

From: Georgeous

To: Shawna B.

Subject: standing offer?

i'm gonna take you up on your offer, just for a bit.

i'd much rather land and come home to you than deal with my mom.

she's a worrier. the apple doesn't fall far from the tree. and i don't think she'll dig my new penchant for percocet.

i hope that's still cool?

will send my flight details, when i have them.

with love,

g

ps my ribs are still sore, so you have to be careful if we…

She writes me back instantly.

From: Shawna B.

To: Georgeous

Subject: YES!!!

Please come! I will pick you up!

All of this near-death stuff has really gotten to me!

Oh my god, I'm writing like one of those girls that ends every sentence with exclamation points.

I love you so much.

Let me know if you need anything.

Shawna

PS Doctor's outfit already purchased. I was going to suggest we play Naughty Nurse, but the heels that came with that outfit were awful.

11

All a woman really wants from you:
> *Respect me.*
> *Make me feel beautiful.*
> *Let me criticize my family,*
> *but never do it yourself.*
> *Be assertive, but know when to listen.*

Bags almost packed, I come across Shawna's first aid kit. I stick it in the duffle and start to zip, then stop. I take it out and leave it on the windowsill. I'm sure Shawna has Band-Aids. And someone here will need them more than me.

I'm so restless. I keep checking my email to postpone the last of the packing. Shawna must be restless, too. I check my email again. There she is.

From: Shawna B.

To: Georgeous

Subject: Soft landing

I am so excited for you to come home! I can't sit still! I'd kill to run an errand for you. Please, please, please? Or even just to know what you are craving to eat? For when you land? You know my cooking is horrible, but I'd love to sit and map alternative routes to whatever you're craving from LAX, based on varying traffic scenarios (I am literally that bored).

CAN YOU TELL I AM EXCITED?

Love,

Shawna

PS No, I'm not wearing sassy doctor's uniform to the airport.

PPS Or am I?

From: Georgeous

To: Shawna B.

Subject: restlessness makes the heart grow fonder?

sassy doctor? so many 'take my temperature' jokes…but all of them terrible.

i am excited to come home. seriously. i'm also kinda anxious about it. but i can't figure out why. no matter. mexican food cures all. and that's what i want for my first stateside meal—a super deluxe burrito from lbj's. i haven't had a fresh tortilla in a year.

see you soon, sweetie.

i love you.

g

"George?"

"Tsviks? Goddamn, you scared me." I look down at my bags. "I'm almost packed."

"You should read. PJ family? The attorney…look."

He hands me an opened FedEx envelope. Our household alone has kept the Panamanian express delivery business afloat.

It's a bunch of stuff I've seen before. Death certificate, PJ's birth certificate, etc. Peter James Ferdinands. I can hear him introducing himself as "Petah," briefly, when we first met—only to quickly correct it with, "But all of my mates call me PJ, ay?"

Fuck, I miss him.

But there's more. A letter from another attorney and a mention of PJ's *estate*. What a joke.

And another birth certificate.

Charlotte, a baby girl.

•

In my last few hours on Bocas, I scour the internet like a fiend. Flights, Google Maps, tourist visa requirements. Tsvika is doing…what? I have no idea. He's on the phone, cranking out the Hebrew like it's his job. Wait, it is his job. It's a treat to hear him speak fluently. But he maintains his stern just-the-facts tone. I guess I'll miss him, too.

Creepy spit-bubble blower.

I haul my bags out to the dock.

Tsvika, my now half friend, half secretary, is giving me a ride into town to catch my flight in his new boat.

"Tsviks, she's beautiful. Cuts the ride time in half. So smooth. What are you gonna name her?"

"I know this is tradition. But I don't know. Supposed to be the playing on the words, yes?"

I look at my overstuffed duffle. It's mostly PJ's t-shirts, protectively wrapped around his cremains. I couldn't bear to part with them, and they're serving the perfect, albeit sad, purpose. Thinking of PJ and his love for puns, the potential boat name hits me.

"For the name, how about *Not for Sail?* But sail like sailboat?"

"Ah, OK. Yes. Good."

Looking at the water, I start saying goodbye to Bocas.

It's bittersweet. Rushed.

Then the note I wrote to Shawna fifteen minutes ago replays in my head.

From: Georgeous

To: Shawna B.

Subject: LAX—not yet

hey sweetie—

i'm a little pressed for time, but you don't need to pick me up at LAX. i need to do a couple things first.

long story.

more later.

love,

g

She doesn't need to pick me up, because I'm heading to PJ's funeral. In Australia. And to find his daughter.

•••

Acknowledgments

I respect, admire and love the people of Panama. George felt that way, and I do too.

A heartfelt thank you to my brilliant editor Maddy Hutchison, who is very talented and an inspiration as a human being.

John (JR) Rogers helped tremendously as a script architect and hand-delivered the first completed manuscript of Bocas to my little spot in Panama.

My writing coach, Pilar Alessandra, gives tough love with grace.

A big bear hug to Toby Petersen, for his acerbic wit and virtuoso design acumen.

David Henstock delivers the goods. Full stop. Spoon you so hard, brother.

Gabe Becker provides motivation and questionable advice. GRUNNY!

I am very grateful for Jennifer Lewis's incredible edits and insight, especially on the feminine perspective.

Glenn Allen is the COO of my life and the most generous and helpful person I know.

Kelley Coyne and Tiny Telephone were wonderful and highly competent during the audio recording.

Alice Yom helps me balance clutter with content and is excellent at shooting lasers. Pew Pew Pew!

Thank you to everyone who weathered early drafts, printed countless versions and provided inspiration. I am forever grateful.

A long, yet still too short list of people I am indebted to—likely with misspellings:

Alexis Clarke, Amber Robinson, Andrew Goldstein, Anna Kim, Archana Chand, Ashley Huck, Ben Smalley, Bethany Letiecq, Blair Harris, Blythe Graham-Jones, Brian Kieley, Brian Sanford, Brian Tymann, Brooke Johnson, Bryan Smith, Caitlin Chu, Carlos Cantu, Carol Kruger, Celina Pham, Charisse Lee, Christine No, Colin Kehn, Craig Wright, Dan Savage, Dave Sixt, David Ferst, David Granger, David Kennedy, David LeCompte, David Ory, David Powell, Doug Deibert, Drew Hopkins, Ed Abbott, Eddie Lopez, Edward Lodens, Elaine Ng, Elissa Klaus, Elizabeth Finkel, Elizabeth Thomas, Ellen Moller, Emma Cunningham, Eric Flynn, Eric Pearsall, Eric Simundza, Eryc Branham, Garth Petersen, Glenn Allen, Greg Miller, Gregory Holmes, Gretel Kearney, Griff Abbott, Gwen Ma, Heather Ryberg, Hilary Clarke, Holly Lorincz, Hugh Gurin, Ian Hill, Ilda Dinis, Ildiko Polony, Ingrid Greene, Jacob Kennedy, Janelle Haskell, Jason Keffer, Jason LoGuidice, Jay Rosenthal, Jaycie Moller, Jennifer Hoggatt, Jennifer Miller, Jeff Norburn, Jeffrey Lutsey, Jessica Dudley, Jill Coy, Jodi Linker, John Zaremba, Johnny Irwin, Jonathan Sprague, Joseph Chang, Joseph Pham, Kar Johnson, Karen Sixt, Katherine Bent, Kandace Karcher, Ken Robinson, Kelsy Reitz, Kerri Danega, Kimberly Spiegelberg, Kristen Johnson, Kristin Spoon, Lance Karnan, Laura Donald, Lauren Ziemski, Lela Beauchene, Lisa Dimaggio, Lisa Kennedy, Liz Branham, Mary Levins, Matt Dill, Matthew Matthew Cordasco, Pinna, Megan Fisher, Melissa Biedler, Melissa Freeman, Meredith Altenhofen, Michel Natalis, Michele Janes, Mike Figueroa,

Monica Bishop, Natasha Zvenigorodsky, Nate Robinson, Nicholas Lutsey, Nicholas Vetter, Nivan Bhuta, Olivia VanDamme, Pablo Monzon, Pamela Koo, Paris Daniell, Peter LeCompte, Phillipa Healy, Rafael Montoya, Remy Savin, Richard Steele, Robert Bryant, Rosetta Jones, Ryan Kelly, Ryan McCarthy, Ryan McGinn, Scott Tansey, Seema Patel, Sharon Ferdinands, Sharon Lim, Simone Slykhous, Soren Kaplan, Steve Cox, Sue Adams, Taylor Baloy, Tony Righetti, The Curros, The Pratts, The Robinsons, The Wentkers, Tim Richards, Tracy Terway, Trinh Tran, Tsvika Tal, Tyler Munson, Vicky Thanh and Vish Shastry.

I was heavily influenced by these works and revere these writers: Don Winslow (Power of the Dog), John Irving (A Prayer for Owen Meany), Jonathan Franzen (The Corrections), Kurt Vonnegut (anything), Lydia Millet (Ghost Lights), Milan Kundera (anything), Pat Barker (Regeneration), Robert Bingham (Lightning on the Sun) and Seth Greenland (The Bones).

Thank you for your help and incredible hospitality: 1760, Al Natural Resort, Anchor Steam, Aqua Lounge, Balboa Beer, Bar Bom Bom, blue rubber bands from Whole Foods, Café Meuse, Common Sage, Crave, Dunya, Enjoy Cupcakes, Esquire Magazine, Flying Pirates, Gasser's Lounge, Hotel Almar Capurgana, Hotel Don Chicho, James Coffee Company, La Barracuda, La Iguana, Lilli's, Maneframe Salon, Maricuya, Metro 3 second floor Hewlett Packard printer at Visa Inc., Mondo Taitu, Paki Point, Papito, Phlox Commons, Playa Bluff Lounge, PW.org, Spinnerie, Staples Express Copy Center on Van Ness, the binder clips I accidentally steal from gyro, The Bookstore, The

Casbah, The Firefly, The House of Chi, The JCC, The Wine Bar, The Wreck Deck, The YMCA and Ultimo Refugio.

About the Author

Thomas M. Barron is a strategist and copywriter. He lives in San

Francisco with his sleepy dog, King. Bocas is his first novel.

CPSIA information can be obtained
at www.ICGtesting.com
Printed in the USA
BVHW031940180421
605255BV00010B/502

9 780999 703342